If...
then

a collection of erotic romance stories

Emerald

If... Then: a collection of erotic romance stories
Copyright © 2014 Emily McCay, writing as Emerald
Published by 1001 Nights Press
Edited by Sharazade
Cover design by CoverDomme

ISBN-13: 978-0692296400
ISBN-10: 0692296409

Table of Contents

Table of Contents

If...

I breezed through the screen door in a breathless whirl. "I brought the tablecloths," I said to the bride's mother, who was busy assembling hors d'oeuvres at the kitchen counter. I set the bag from the store on the dining room table already cluttered with picnic paraphernalia – except for tablecloths, which Sarah had called in a frenzy to tell me her mother had forgotten to pick up.

"Great," Sarah's mom said as she turned from the counter and gave me a hug. "Here's your nametag. Would you mind being in charge of handing those out?"

"Not at all," I said, shuffling through the stack as I stepped back out onto the deck. I peeled the back off mine, labeled with my name and "Maid of Honor" in smaller letters below it, and pressed it to my dress.

"Hey Valerie," Sarah called behind me as I reached the wooden steps. I turned as she emerged from the house and met me in a hug. "Where's Chris?"

"He wasn't feeling well this morning. He wanted me to tell you and Shawn he's really sorry to miss your engagement party."

"I'm sorry to hear that. Tell him I hope he feels better soon. No big deal though about today," Sarah continued with a wave of her hand as we headed down the steps to the backyard. "This is really just to introduce the wedding party and Shawn's and my extended family to each other before all the wedding stuff starts in earnest, you know?"

I nodded as Sarah continued on to find Shawn while I veered toward the front of the house to commence my job. The guests started to arrive, and I greeted them at the driveway and directed them with their nametags to the picnic tables in the backyard. As one of the groomsmen I knew and his wife approached, I handed them their nametags before turning to the man with them.

"I'm Hayden – the best man," he said with a smile. He slipped his sunglasses off to reveal the friendly slate-gray eyes below his tousled dark hair.

"Oh, yes, I remember seeing your name in here somewhere." I gave him a quick smile, feeling a bit flustered as I shuffled through the stack in my hands. I knew next to nothing about the best man, except that I would be walking down the aisle with him in about six months... and that I found my face burning at the idea. Unnerved by this response, I located his nametag and handed it to him.

"Thanks," he said easily. I kept my voice light as I directed the three of them to the yard, a vague heat forming in my belly as I noted the lack of a ring on Hayden's left hand.

I turned back toward the driveway, recalling with a deep breath that I myself *was* spoken for. My eyes dropped as guilt replaced the excitement stirring in me. Chris and I weren't married, but we had been together for three years, and even if I had been feeling inexplicably restless and confused lately, I was still monogamously committed to him.

When the last nametag had been handed out, I went to the dessert table. In a rare indulgence, I allowed myself a piece of cake and carried it to the circle of chairs occupied mostly by the bridal party. I took the empty seat directly across from Hayden and did my best to ignore the fluttering in my stomach as I turned my attention to the cake on my plate.

It was dark chocolate, with a layer of raspberries in the middle and creamy white frosting on top. I scooped up a dollop of frosting and gave it a delicate lick as I listened to Sarah talk about invitations. Nodding periodically in response to her monologue, I ran my tongue over my frosting-sweetened lips and glanced up to see Hayden watching me.

I blushed and looked down – though not before I caught the deliberate interest beneath his cool gaze. Breathless, I turned my attention back to Sarah as confusion formed in my core. Why was I having such a response to Hayden? I was in a monogamous relationship. Much as I would have jumped on this opportunity years ago when that wasn't the case, I was in no position to do so now.

When Sarah paused in her description, I jumped up and dropped my plate in the trash on the way to the food table to grab something to take inside. I didn't look back as I headed with both hands full toward the house. On the way up the wooden steps to the deck, I climbed too quickly and slipped, nearly dropping the Crockpot in my hands before I felt a firm grasp around my waist from behind.

"Easy," Hayden's voice said in my ear, and I got wet. It may be that I wasn't supposed to, but I did.

I steadied myself and turned around. Hayden's hands slipped from my waist, and he smiled.

I cleared my throat. "Thank you. Can I get something for you inside?"

"No, I'm just heading to the restroom. Let me get that for you." He reached in front of me for the screen door.

"Thank you," I said again, aware of the adrenaline zinging through me as I set the Crockpot on the counter. I bit my lip as I stood still for a moment. I wondered if the fact that I felt utterly forbidden from touching – much less fucking the hell out of, which was what I really wanted to do – Hayden was influencing how desperately I felt like I wanted to.

I went to the guest bedroom and sent Chris a text message, eager to lock myself away from people for a few moments. I waited for his reply informing me that he was feeling better before I left the room, trying not to think about Hayden happening to wander in and catch me there. As I headed back outside, I felt very grateful that he didn't.

Didn't I?

Slowly the guests began to take their leave. The sun had turned a dark orange on the horizon, the sky overhead the color of smoke when I grabbed a round of gifts from a table to take inside. A few people had begun to congregate on the deck, and as I approached the wooden steps, Hayden broke away and came down them.

"It was a pleasure meeting you, Valerie," he said with a smile.

"Are you leaving?" My voice managed to stay light despite the tug I felt inside when Hayden nodded.

"Well, I would hug you if I wasn't all loaded down," I laughed as I neared him, indicating the wine bottle-laden gift bags filling my hands and feeling a wistful pull at the missed opportunity.

Hayden hadn't paused, and even as I spoke he reached me, his arm sliding seamlessly around my waist as my words evaporated. I caught my breath as he held my lower back lightly while I pressed against him for a moment.

I turned my head and barely brushed my lips against his cheek as I stepped back.

"There, I'll kiss you instead," I said, surprised by how unaffected my voice sounded.

Hayden's chuckle was barely audible. "That wasn't a kiss."

Barely moving forward, his lips touched mine so lightly it was possible those behind him on the deck wouldn't even know what was happening in the shadowy dusk around us. He backed up with the same silence with which he had moved forward.

My breath had seemed to disappear into the growing darkness. Though I stood stock still, my lungs surged for air as I sought my voice, which seemed to have dissolved as well. Finally a whisper came out.

"Hayden."

His eyebrows rose.

The fixation in me seemed to snap, and I smiled, suddenly feeling clearer. "I want to let you know that I find myself, um, quite attracted to you."

This seemed a laughable understatement, but I stayed focused. Hayden's intense gaze was fixed on me. It showed nothing to discourage the disclosure.

"Desperately so, in fact," I continued. My eyes flicked to the ground, then back up to his. "And I am not in a position to act on that at this time. Otherwise, I would have done so already."

Hayden's expression cleared, and I could see he didn't have to ask questions.

I backed up. Exhaling slowly, I said, "It was a pleasure meeting you too, Hayden. I guess I'll see you at the wedding."

He stepped away as well and smiled. "Yes. You certainly will."

He gave a wave as he turned and headed for his car. I hoisted the gift bags and walked up the wooden steps to the deck, my stomach churning, head whirling, and pussy dripping.

I found Chris on the couch under a blanket when I walked in the front door.

"How was the party?" he asked before I could say anything.

"Uh, fine," I answered. Did my voice betray me? My stomach clenched, and I reminded myself I hadn't done anything wrong.

I looked in Chris's beautiful blue eyes. I loved him so much. I had made a decision to be with him, and that was what I wanted.

Wasn't it?

"How are you feeling?" I asked, moving to sit at his side.

He sat up a little. "Better. You're beautiful." He smiled at me as he moved a wisp of hair from my face. His expression segued into concern. "What's wrong?"

I had barely noticed the tears filling my eyes. I shook my head dismissively and stood up.

"I'm going upstairs to change. Can I get you anything?"

"No, thank you," Chris said, still watching me as he eased back against the couch. "I love you."

"I love you too." I pulled the blanket over him and smiled, leaning down to kiss his cheek before I turned and left the room.

Upstairs, I pulled off my dress and slipped out of my sandals. Why did the complication of Hayden have to come right at this time? I had been feeling unsettled and uncertain for the past several weeks as it was.

Maybe that was why.

Standing in my thong, I thought of Hayden and caught my breath. I could almost feel his hands on my waist from behind, the confidence of his arm sliding around me in the darkness. I swallowed.

Quietly I crept to the door and closed it, then slipped off my thong and eased onto the bed. I spread my legs and remembered what little contact Hayden and I had had at the party, surprised by the force of the arousal that resulted. I dropped my fingers between my legs.

Breathing heavily, I pressed my clit, remembering the way Hayden's arm had slid around me without pause, the breath-like feeling of his lips touching mine, the hunger in his eyes when I caught him watching me lick the white creamy frosting. I was astonished by how easily I came thinking of nothing else. Twice.

I closed my eyes and imagined Hayden finding me in the guest bedroom. I could almost feel his tongue circling one nipple, then the other as he pulled my clothes off before pushing me onto the bed, shoving my legs apart as I begged him to fuck me hard.

All together I made myself come six times. As I got up shakily and headed for the shower, my eyes fell on the nametag still stuck to the dress crumpled on the floor. My insides twisted as I remembered that what had just happened with Hayden in my fantasies could remain only there.

Two weeks later I woke in the middle of the night. Blinking sleepily, I glanced at the moonlight penetrating the blackness out the window and didn't bother checking the clock. I looked at Chris, his breathing even as he lay on his side, facing me, his hands balled into fists just under the edge of the blanket.

I had been thinking about Hayden alarmingly frequently in the weeks since I'd met him. It had been a bit surreal to feel something so all-encompassing that Chris had no idea about. I found the juxtaposition uncomfortable, and I had a sad feeling that Chris had no idea anything was wrong. Of course, while I knew that *something* was, I had no idea what. And it had been there, I knew, even before I met Hayden.

I shifted my head on the pillow and smothered a sigh. The idea of leaving Chris, leaving the relationship, seemed startling to me, and I didn't feel at all certain that was what I wanted. But why was I so captivated by Hayden?

I flipped onto my stomach and faced the other direction. Moments later I felt the bed shift and was about to turn my head when I felt Chris's form against my side, his lips dropping to the back of my neck and moving steadily to my ear. I was shocked by the goosebumps that immediately stood all over my body, by how quickly the confusion that had just seemed so paramount fell under the heat of Chris's touch.

For a split second I felt compelled to contemplate that, but Chris made his way on top of me, his erection pressing against my ass, and distraction evaporated. He didn't say anything, just reached up and gave my hair a little tug as my whimper got lost in the pillow. His lips nuzzled my ear, then moved across my cheek and finally barely reached my lips, which he kissed lightly before returning to the intense erogenous zone of my ear.

I heard the condom wrapper and felt him shift briefly and then slip inside me, my legs together, still face down flat on the bed. Chris moved his hands to my shoulders, fucking me with a slow rhythm that seemed to fit the silence and the moonlight and the middle of the night like a door clicking quietly shut.

My eyes closed, body pressed against the mattress, I basked in the heavy warmth of Chris's weight and his cock sliding in and out of me. I gripped his fingers as he covered my hands with his on the pillow, and he squeezed back before letting go to slide one hand under my body. I came silently and quickly, the only outward indications the audible quickening of my breath and the increased pressure of my body against the mattress and Chris's fingers.

Chris came silently too, his grip on my shoulder tightening. When it was done, he reached to kiss me again, and I smiled sleepily, my eyes still closed. Chris slid off me, curling his arm around mine and pulling me into a spooning position. For a split second I felt his grip tighten in the darkness, and I had the instantaneous sense that my suspicion of his obliviousness had been misplaced. I blinked my eyes open as the grasp relaxed and I heard Chris's breathing return to the steadiness indicating sleep.

Letting go of any attempt to grapple things into making sense, I took a deep breath and followed suit.

Shopping for bridesmaid dresses with Sarah the following weekend, I noticed that anything having to do with the wedding seemed to be reminding me of Hayden. I sighed as I zipped up the A-line burgundy dress and stepped out of the dressing room.

Sarah cocked her head. "Hmmm. That's nice." Her brow furrowed. "Could I see the blue one again?"

I smiled, amused by her indecision. I had tried each of her three final dress choices twice; this would be the third time for the blue one. I ducked back into the dressing room and slipped on the royal blue floor-length strapless gown. She looked up as I emerged.

"I like that," she said as she examined me. "Do you like that one or the short black one better?"

"For a winter wedding, longer seems to make sense," I responded. "Though it's up to you, of course."

Sarah nodded thoughtfully. "Oh, by the way, I asked Shawn to meet us here at two-thirty to go to the tuxedo store down the street. I want to look at the tuxes that match the dresses I'm looking at. Do you mind coming with to give your opinion?"

"Of course not." I returned to the dressing room to change back into my street clothes. As I stepped into my shoes, I heard voices outside the door and deduced that Shawn had arrived.

I opened the door, and my breath caught as I saw Shawn talking to Sarah – with Hayden standing next to him. My heart took off like a pistol firing, and for a second I couldn't speak.

Sarah turned to me. "Shawn brought Hayden with him, obviously. You guys met at the engagement party, right?" Shawn said something to her before I could answer, and she turned to him.

Hayden stood casually, his hands in the pockets of his khakis. I met his eyes, his slow smile shooting sparks through my body. I swallowed and managed a somewhat unnatural smile back.

Sarah and Shawn started toward the door, and I snapped out of my daze long enough to thank the salesperson that had helped us before the four of us exited the store. The bride and groom fell into step with each other, leaving Hayden and me together behind them.

The intense attraction I still felt toward Hayden was undeniable. Guilt flooded through me as we made small talk, and I wondered if my voice sounded as stilted to him as it did to me. I also wondered if what had seemed to be his mutual interest was still there, or if what I had said at the party had – understandably, admittedly – erased it.

It had obviously had no such effect on me.

As we entered the formalwear store I held back a groan, suddenly realizing that if there was one thing I didn't need the temptation of seeing Hayden in right now, it was a tuxedo. I looked around and tried to quell the simmering in my stomach as Sarah talked to the salesperson. After a brief interim of vest- and tie-collecting, Shawn and Hayden disappeared down the hallway to the changing rooms.

Moments later they both emerged in tuxes, and my insides melted a bit. My cunt actually grew wet at the sight of Hayden in his black tuxedo and silver vest. There was a brief discussion of colors, during which I hoped my silence wasn't conspicuous, before the two men went back down the hall.

Looking at Hayden had reminded me of how I felt when I saw the decadent chocolate desserts in the bakery section of the grocery store: I was so used to depriving myself that it didn't even occur to me to buy one – I simply looked at them longingly, and every once in a while I found myself startled by the sudden and violent urge to throw aside the glass door and shove one in my mouth before I could change my mind.

"Sarah, can you give me a hand with this?" Shawn called from his dressing room.

Sarah disappeared down the hall, and reluctantly I followed her. I settled on the chair near the three-way mirror as Sarah slipped into Shawn's changing room.

Another door opened, and Hayden stepped out in the same tuxedo with a dark red vest and tie that I recognized as matching the burgundy dress I had just tried on. I stared for a moment before realizing it would be polite to acknowledge his presence rather than just salivate over it. I looked up at him and managed a smile.

"What do you think?" he asked.

I bit back exactly what I thought, which was that I wanted to fuck him senseless.

"It looks lovely," I said. "Actually..." I tried to stop myself, but my body seemed to move of its own accord as I stood and straightened his slightly crooked bow tie.

"That's better," I murmured.

The heat of his body was like a magnet – and I a helpless paper clip – as I pulled back with supreme effort. His steel-gray eyes held mine, and confusion and uncertainty suddenly flooded through me so strongly my eyes almost filled with tears. I took another step back.

As I did, Hayden caught my arm, pulling me into the changing room and pushing me against the wall in a single movement. His mouth was on mine before I had time to catch my breath, much less remember to resist. My body pressed into his, cradling the erection I felt beneath his trousers.

A whimper escaped me, and abruptly I broke away, my pussy wet and throbbing as I stumbled to the other side of the tiny dressing room. I braced my hands against the wall, silently trying to catch my breath. Behind me I heard Hayden doing the same.

"I'm sorry," he whispered. I turned back to him. "Really. I know you told me. I just found you...irresistible."

Well, I certainly knew the feeling. He looked down, and I didn't doubt his contriteness. I nodded at him, near tears. I had come very close to crossing a line.

Hayden cleared his throat and touched my arm as he opened the door for me. "I'm very sorry, Valerie."

I smiled feebly to let him know it was all right – I knew it wasn't all his fault, after all – and passed through to the hallway.

Shawn and Sarah emerged momentarily, and I jumped. I barely noticed the conversation around me as I resisted meeting Hayden's eyes. To do so felt like it would threaten my resistance of the violent urge to push him right back into the dressing room and shove him in my mouth before I could change my mind.

When I got home, I once again found myself fantasizing incessantly about Hayden. Chris was out, and I lay on the bed and pictured Hayden and me the day of the wedding, hidden in one of the preparation rooms after the ceremony as I knelt and sucked his cock, his breathing frantic above me as he stood in his shiny black dress shoes and ebony tuxedo, shoving his hips forward and grasping the back of my head.

His ceaseless pumping into my mouth would make my pussy drip, and I'd look up at his silver eyes locked on mine and let him know that as much as I loved what I was doing, I was going to demand that he take my pussy before he was done. I came to the image of the shiny blue satin dress bunched at my hips as Hayden drilled into me from behind.

I caught my breath before I stood and headed for the closet. *Who knows what will be going on come winter, when the wedding is?* I mused absently. Maybe by then we would have the chance.

When I realized what I had just thought, I stopped short, my breath catching. Shock enveloped me as I realized I had just caught myself nonchalantly considering not being with Chris anymore. What was I thinking? That was a huge change my mind was throwing around, not some casual consideration. How could the idea have slid through my consciousness so easily?

Tears pushed up from my core as I met my gaze in the mirror across the room. Staring at my reflection, I jumped as I heard the door open downstairs.

Chris was home.

I had been making omelets the Sunday morning Chris walked into the kitchen and told me he knew something was wrong.

At that moment, I knew he had known all along. Starting before I met Hayden, back to the weeks prior when something had seemed off, when I hadn't known what it was or whether it was he or I or both or neither, just that it was something, Chris had known. He had always known.

He'd stood facing me, and I'd turned to him. And told him everything. I told him about meeting Hayden, about the day in the dressing room, about how guilty and uncertain and overwhelmed I felt, about how it had started even before then but I didn't know why.

Chris had listened silently, and I found that just sharing it, speaking the words out loud, seemed to open something in me. A relaxation I hadn't felt for months flowed over me.

And when he'd said he had felt me pulling away for months and not known why or what to do, I realized what had eluded me for so long: What was happening in me wasn't about Chris, and it wasn't about Hayden. Not deep down.

It was about me.

Chris and I had reached a turning point. The relationship was asking me for something I had never given before. It was asking me to go deeper – deeper trust, deeper authenticity, deeper surrender.

It was asking me for intimacy.

The request was quiet, so subtle that I had only recognized it subconsciously. And there was a part of me that was afraid of it. That part, the part that had avoided it so many times before in my life, was loud, and it used whatever it needed to distract me.

Enter Hayden and the incredible, magnetic sexual attraction of avoidance.

The attraction I felt to Hayden was sincere, I didn't doubt. But I saw then that the fixation I had experienced around him was an unconscious redirection of my attention. It was the loud, fearful part of me employing a strategy to direct my awareness away from what it found so threatening. Because ultimately it wasn't about intimacy with another person. It was about intimacy with myself.

Looking at Chris that day, I had understood that for me, the intimacy had always been harder. Harder than leaving and starting over again, only reaching a certain level before I found something new that carried an intensity that magnetically called to me. I felt the intensity with Hayden, for sure. I had felt it many times in my life. And while at that moment I saw the pattern that had played out over and over in my past relationships when I resisted calls to go deeper and went after what was new instead, I saw as well that at those times, I wasn't ready for it yet. The precision of this opportunity was unique – unique to here, unique to now, unique to this.

And as always, I still had the option to turn it down.

When winter came, the bushes outside the reception venue topped by domes of smooth white snow, I entered the room on Hayden's arm. The bridal party followed behind us as we made our way to the head table amidst the excited chatter of the 100+ guests.

Hayden pulled my chair out for me, and I smiled as I thanked him and released his arm. He gave me a wink and turned to find his seat on the other side of Shawn's. I watched him, recalling the various fantasies I'd entertained about the two of us on this day. The attraction was still there. Had I been at liberty to, I would have fucked Hayden silly every chance I'd had. I would have jumped him in the guest bedroom at Sarah and Shawn's engagement party, I would have sucked his cock in the dressing room of the men's formalwear store, I would have dragged him off for a quickie in one of the back rooms prior to the ceremony that had just taken place.

As it was, I was not at liberty to. I arranged my belongings under my chair and stood to dismount the platform, holding up my royal blue floor-length dress with one hand as I descended the steps and crossed the dance floor.

Chris met me at the edge of it. He stepped forward to kiss me, and my dress swished around my ankles as I dropped it to wrap my arms around his neck.

"I have to go back to the head table," I whispered. "I just wanted to say hi and I'll see you as soon as the first dances are over."

Chris ran a finger along my jaw, sending a shiver down my back as his hand rested suggestively on my hip. I suspected he was thinking of the new fantasy I had shared with him before he had dropped me off earlier for photos. It was cold outside, and I doubted anyone else would venture out and find us behind the building, my hands planted against the wall and Chris's cock buried deep inside me.

Though as I had also told him, I recalled as I kissed him a final time and turned back toward the platform, I didn't mind if it remained just a fantasy either. From across the room, Hayden's silver gaze met mine as I gathered my dress and started to return to the head table. I had certainly developed an appreciation for the value of fantasy – even if it was never acted out.

Soft and Gray

"Kate, I'm sorry. I didn't mean anything."

Kate looked at him. Her eyes were as hard as the steel their color matched. "But you said it. Why would you have said it if you didn't mean it?"

Kate's voice was even, leveling the cold, scathing anger that worked from an impersonal objectivity that was chilling. One thoughtless remark could catch its razor-sharp attention; like an unremitting lawyer, Kate noticed little slip-ups, however meaningless they seemed on the part of their perpetrator. It wouldn't even have to have anything to do with herself, as evidenced by this instance. The anger in her operated on a higher level – its only standard was an uncompromising self-righteousness.

He had meant nothing by it. But there was nothing that meant nothing to Kate.

"Kate..." Aaron's voice failed as her gaze sliced through him.

"The excuse of thoughtlessness isn't good enough this time."

She disappeared through the doorway in three strides, her footsteps audible on the marble floor of the foyer. She didn't go out the front door. He heard her continue to another room. In this mansion, they both knew it could take him all night to find her. Furthermore, it was her parents' house – she knew he wasn't going to go wandering off on his own looking for her.

He heard voices in the foyer and surmised that Ralph and his girlfriend Bethany were coming home from the baseball game. Ralph, six years Kate's junior, had just graduated from high school and was still living at home. They entered the front room, where Aaron still stood between the doorway and the fireplace, and flopped down on the couch. Aaron had never thought of it as a couch to "flop down" on, with its immaculate velvet cushions and curved wooden arms and legs. Granted, his memories of other things he and Kate had done on it also seemed to defy that impression.

Aaron tuned out Bethany's enthusiastic account of the game until she sat up and directed a greeting toward the doorway. He turned to see Kate, and his breath caught. She didn't look at him, and her expression didn't change as she said hello.

"So what are you guys doing here? Where are Mom and Dad?" Ralph asked.

"Dad is in his office. Mom is around somewhere. We came by to drop something off and stayed for dinner."

Ralph raised his eyebrows at Kate's controlled monotony. "And how are you this evening?" he asked with all the sarcasm of an eighteen-year-old.

Kate's steel-gray eyes shifted to his. She didn't answer.

"What have you got your panties in a twist about now?" Ralph drawled, and Aaron winced internally. It had often seemed to him that Ralph was one of the few people not at all intimidated by the solid ice of Kate's anger when she perceived wrongdoing. Bethany nudged her boyfriend with a frown, but he continued. "When are you going to learn to lighten up, Katie? Your eyes look like bullets. Why can't they ever look like – what's something soft and gray?" He appealed to Bethany.

Soft and gray. Aaron had seen them look that way many times.

Bethany looked at Ralph dubiously, and he turned back to Kate. "Anyway, you need to loosen up." He stood up, and Bethany followed. "We'll get out of your way."

"Don't bother." Kate whirled, and Aaron heard her cross the wide foyer again. She wore sneakers, but the marble floor hid the sound of no shoe's sole. The quick squeaks grew fainter, and then subsided.

"What's her problem?" Ralph turned to Aaron.

Aaron shook his head and looked at the carpet where it met the black swirled marble of the foyer floor. There was silence until the chords of a piano reached them from somewhere far away in the house.

"Oh, Kate's playing," Bethany said, sounding relieved by the distraction. "Let's go listen to her." She started toward the doorway, and Ralph followed. Glancing back at Aaron, he said, "Are you coming?"

Aaron shook his head. He sensed Ralph about to question, then turn and continue through the door. The soles of four shoes thumped on the marble, soon joined by the clacking of Kate's mother's high heels in route to some unknown location in the mansion.

Aaron stayed where he was, his eyes moving to the volume of Shakespeare bound in brown leather on the coffee table. The Complete Works, he read in shiny gold letters across the cover. The volume had sat on that same table, in this same room – the one in which he'd by far spent the most time in this house – for the two years he'd been coming here. Only once had he seen it moved.

There were instances when the guardedness that seemed to hold such fort in Kate came down. He remembered the time they had come to see her parents and found them not at home. As they'd sat in this room, waiting, Kate had picked up the volume he stared at now. He'd listened while she read out loud from The Taming of the Shrew, her favorite Shakespeare piece, her voice filling the air with reverence and something else.

He had been shocked when she had abruptly put the book down and stripped off her shirt and bra. Before he could even say anything, she'd yanked his jeans open and lunged for his cock, which was immediately hard. She sucked with the enthusiasm of a master performer on the highest stage, never breaking to say a word as she swallowed his cock over and over, taking it deep into her throat as his shock turned to arousal combined with the exhilarating uncertainty of when her parents might come home. Without pulling her mouth from him, she'd grabbed his shirt and jerked him into a standing position, presumably so she could sit back and take the come he soon shot all over her face, licking it ravenously from her lips and rubbing it across her breasts and back up her throat before sucking each of her fingers dry.

The genius of Shakespeare, she'd later explained, turned her on.

Aaron's gaze shifted to the wall. Kate's parents loved Edgar Allan Poe's "The Raven" so much they'd commissioned it to be copied in calligraphy for display. It took two huge frames that hung side by side, their golden ornateness offering a focal point in this cove of artistic luxury. Aaron traced the intricate lettering with his gaze, as if he were writing it with his eyes. He remembered studying it the same way the first time he'd been in this house, the night he had met her parents for the first time. The four of them had had a formal dinner before Kate's parents departed for the theater, and prior to eating they had gathered in this room. Aaron had found himself all but transfixed by the exquisite calligraphy depicting the poem.

Kate appeared in the doorway, as Aaron realized he'd been subconsciously expecting ever since the piano strains had changed from those of a talented pianist to Bethany's cheerful chopsticks about two minutes before. Somehow he hadn't heard her shoes on the marble.

He didn't look up right away. He was afraid to.

Instead, his gaze locked itself on the burgundy sofa. Despite his perception of its elegance and formality, he and Kate had wasted no time fucking on it after her parents left for the theater that night. They had returned to this opulent room with a bottle of equally opulent champagne, and he had undressed her and lowered himself on top of her on the luxurious velvet, moving slowly as though to respect the majestic formality of the room.

Despite himself, he grew hard as he remembered how hot she felt when he buried himself inside her, how she eventually tossed her champagne flute aside (a mess she would meticulously clean up later) and climbed onto her knees, her pale skin exquisite against the deep velvet as the order she gave to fuck her from behind made any inclination toward slowness in him disappear. He had fucked her with abandon, ramming into her as she'd climaxed with a shriek, her body draped over the sofa's curved back, tight fists gripping the smooth dark wood.

Kate moved into the room now. Aaron looked at her. He couldn't see her eyes – only her profile and the flutter of the black curve of her eyelashes as she blinked. Aaron slipped his hand in his pocket and ran his index finger along the cropped velvet on the box. It wasn't going to happen tonight. He took a deep, silent breath and focused on the view beyond the window.

Kate paced to the back of the barely lit room, where she was almost lost to him in the shadows. The sky had grown darker in the few minutes Ralph and Bethany had been gone, and a charcoal gloom covered their surroundings. Kate stopped and stared at the oversized hanging of Van Gogh's "Cafe Terrace at Night" on the back wall.

Aaron looked back at the coffee table. The wind whistled quietly through the fireplace.

She turned and faced him from across the room. He looked up, unable to see more than her silhouette in the shadows.

"I will not forgive you this time, Aaron."

Her voice was darker than the room in which he was left standing. Stricken, it took a few seconds of hearing the squeak on marble before he realized he needed to go after her. He took a step out of the room. She was gone.

Fighting the urge to turn around and reenter that which was familiar to him, Aaron turned left and set off across the foyer, bypassing the sweeping staircase for the hallway that ran behind it. He had no idea where Kate would be. Most of his visits to the Buchanan's house had been formal, without much wandering of the countless rooms of the mansion. But the chances were just as good he would run into Kate as either of her parents, and he could always excuse himself if the latter happened. Finding her was more important than politeness.

He quickened his pace, then stopped as he heard a noise. He crept forward, passing a full-length mirror on his right before he came upon the open doorway to the billiard room. Kate was there, quietly pulling a bottle from the wet bar. The glass clinked as it brushed one of its neighbors.

She looked up as he entered. He couldn't see her eyes. Minus the backlight of the bar, there were no lights on in the room. He couldn't tell whether she felt anger at his parading around the house trying to find her or relief that he had done exactly that.

He stopped just inside the doorway. Before he realized what he was doing, his hand reached behind him and pushed the door closed. Kate's shadow didn't move. When he heard the faint latch, he slowly took a step forward and moved around the pool table toward her. She set her drink down. As he got closer, the smoothness of her skin took on a glow in the faint backlight.

Bethany's piano playing started up again. Aaron continued forward and slipped his arm around Kate's waist before he could see her gray eyes clearly. If they looked as they had the last time he'd seen them, he knew he wouldn't have the nerve to touch her.

To Aaron it felt as if her body tried to stiffen but was receiving mixed signals somewhere inside. He pushed his mouth to hers, suddenly breathless with wanting her. Grabbing her with both arms, he twirled her around and lifted her in one movement to the pool table where she sat with her legs wrapped around his waist as he kissed her with a desperation he couldn't remember ever feeling. It didn't have to do with her body, with fucking her. It was just her. Or him. Or both, he couldn't tell. He just knew that the very act of touching her was like an orgasm. Their clothes were all on, and his hands were touching only her waist, and he felt like he was coming – like something was climaxing in him that wasn't sexual but felt just as powerful, as though he couldn't bear to stop touching her.

Kate's lips were kissing him back, but it felt like a moment out of time, like something beyond their actual lives that he couldn't necessarily count on to mean what he wanted it to when it was over. He had seen her body overtake her before, when it was as though it borrowed time from her mind. It didn't mean it wouldn't have to be paid back.

Kate had the highest standards of anyone he had ever met – a strict idealist of an order he had not before encountered. A righteous anger could envelop her over a casual thoughtless comment and an inner fight would seem to take her over, the fierce invisible idealism inside her rising to its most uncompromising severity.

It could be awe-inspiring. Or it could be devastating.

He had no idea which this time would end up being.

"Kate. I love you." The words came from his mouth as it left hers to press the skin of her cheek, her neck, her ear, constantly moving, his hands now clutching her back, pulling her into him. She hadn't made a sound, and he truly didn't know from her body's response what any verbal one might be.

Aaron's breath was uneven as he sensed his declaration couldn't be tempered by any reply she gave right now anyway. Even if he was met with attack, if what he said and did laid him open to vulnerability to a degree that rendered defense nonexistent, what was in him was coming out whether he wanted it to or not. His body shuddered, possibly in fear.

"Marry me. Please," he heard come out of his mouth, and it was as though he was observing, listening to someone else, like he was part of the air, simply watching for the response to the words that had just slipped into the space around them.

He felt her body tense and didn't know what it meant. He kept touching her, as if not even of his own accord, his hands moving to her hips, then around to her ass. He climbed up on the pool table with her, one knee on the hard felt surface at a time as he continued kissing her, continued whispering words he didn't feel like he was in control of saying. His lips pressed along her neck as if magnetically attracted to her skin.

Physically up against her, he could almost feel the fight going on inside her. He didn't know what that was like. Was there anything stronger than an idealism higher than reality?

"God. I love you." It wasn't a plea. It wasn't to convince her. It was just coming, tumbling over the waterfall that was crashing inside him, moving his hands, his body, his voice. He pushed her down on the table, feeling like he needed to be ever closer, as though her body held the air he breathed. She still had not spoken.

Suddenly her body jolted. Aaron froze, backing up as his eyes locked on hers. Even at this close range, he still couldn't see them clearly. He heard her breathing and had trouble with his own as he waited for her to speak.

She didn't – just kept looking, breathing steadily beneath him as he felt her skin against his. There was a shift, though neither of them moved, and Aaron caught his breath as he felt the sudden calmness like the fragrance of a flower, silent and intangible.

Kate's breathing was strong now, moving something he could feel, something beyond words, conveyed through the energy of her body. In the strength he felt a delicacy, and he remembered a phrase Kate herself had used one time, a time she was struggling as she was now, and he hadn't understood what it meant: "the exquisite strength of vulnerability." She had said at the time it was the only thing that could overcome the façade of rigidity – because the illusion of strength in that wasn't real.

He sensed the pinnacle, the climax of the struggle within her. She was fully conscious of what she was doing – this he suddenly knew – and what she did this moment would say what would win. Whether he would ever return here again, or if this interlude in the billiard room would be the last time he would set foot on this grand mansion's marble foyer floor.

His fingers hovered along her skin, and he almost jumped when they brushed the satin between her legs. He stopped and held his breath. Though his hand trembled, he left it there, resting against the fabric between them with the pressure of dew on petals. The position overwhelmed him, and he felt something inside him fully let go. He had no control over what she did. Love was all he could offer.

At that moment he understood what she had meant. Strength and the allowance of vulnerability – somewhere, in a place he had never seen or even conceived of, they were the same thing. Kate had known that already. She had seen it before. He looked at her, feeling something like awe as his fingers trembled against her softness.

Then Kate's legs fell open like a butterfly's wings. Aaron stared, frozen, as she leapt with the grace of a lion and he suddenly found himself on his back, Kate on top of him, fluid as liquid as her body covered his as though in waves as she pulled her shirt off and his mouth literally watered at the sight of her naked breasts.

His body was now at the whim of hers, and he seceded like the sand to the wave. It was not the ravenous lust he had felt in Kate before, like a temporary escape from what held on so tightly inside of her. It was something beyond it altogether, or perhaps including it but so expanded that what had before seemed bigger than life was only a speck in the beauty suspended above him.

Her gaze pulled his eyes to hers. He couldn't see them, but he didn't need to anymore. He could feel what came through them, beyond any words she hadn't yet uttered. Strength, the indivisible surrender to vulnerability, emanated through the darkness from far below their gray surface. It had won.

Aaron began breathing again, knowing even as it formulated that the assessment was erroneous: strength never needed to "win" – it was there, always, inherent in the essence of existence itself whether recognized or not. Strength hadn't won; it hadn't needed to.

But they had.

Honey Changes Everything

Kim wrestled her armload of groceries through the back door and kicked it shut behind her. Setting the bags on the kitchen counter, she glanced at the blinking light on the answering machine and pressed play.

"Kim, it's Maria. I've been meaning to call you. Drake told me about Terry, and I'm so sorry – we both are. I wanted to welcome you to keep in touch, and if there's anything I can do, please let me know." She paused. Kim could picture Maria's blue eyes shining with sincerity, her delicate features emanating concern. "As you may know, Drake's not altogether certain about his job either at this point. Anyway, feel free to give me a call, Kim. Take care."

Kim sighed. She remembered the first time she'd met Maria, the wife of her husband's colleague – former colleague now – Drake, several years ago at the company's annual gala. "Oh my god – your husband looks exactly like Denzel Washington!" had been one of the first things Maria had ever said to her, after their husbands were whisked away for an informal conference immediately following their introduction. She'd giggled, hiccuping a bit as she turned wide eyes back to Kim. "I hope you don't mind my saying that."

Kim had laughed. She'd liked Maria immediately, charmed by the bubbling spunk that seemed somewhat spurred by the glasses of white wine that occupied the petite woman's hand most of the evening. She'd known that what Maria meant, of course, was that she hoped Kim didn't mind that she had just spent the last several seconds ogling her husband. Kim didn't mind, and she'd given Maria a wink as she'd answered, "I know."

Writing herself a note now to call Maria, Kim stuck the Post-It near the phone and turned to unload the bags on the counter. It was Tuesday. The news had come a week ago the previous Friday, when Terry had gone to work as usual with no wisp of an idea that he would return home a few hours later without a job. The layoff was a surprise individually but not collectively in the face of the current economy.

Kim hadn't panicked – it wasn't her style – but the effect it had had on Terry was dramatic. She suspected it was more than concern about their financial well-being, that losing the job he had worked so hard and made his way to second-tier management in for 10 years hurt something inside him he hadn't thought about for a long time. Something he had taken for granted, that external circumstances had allowed to be latent. If Kim was right, though, it wasn't about anything external.

She felt her stomach tighten as she put away the groceries. The financial implications, of course, would soon make themselves known. They would be okay for this month, and probably the next. After that was uncertain. Her own catering business, which she ran from home, had been affected by the economy as well, and though it had been fairly successful in its three-year life, it wasn't enough to support them both.

Kim pulled open the refrigerator door, her ebony ringlets swaying like silent wind chimes in the reflection of its gleaming surface. Catching sight of a smudge as she closed it, she reached for the glass cleaner just as she heard Terry coming down the stairs.

Turning, she saw him enter the living room. She knew he had been upstairs on the computer, most likely searching through jobs or working on his resume. He shuffled forward onto the linoleum.

"Want some lunch?" she asked.

Terry shook his head, not looking at her as he sorted through the stack of papers beside the phone. Kim watched him, unsure what to say. She couldn't say everything would be okay, because she didn't know that it would. She couldn't tell him not to be scared, because she was too.

She lowered her head with a frown, suspecting again that the demon Terry was wrestling went deeper than those things. Something in him questioned more than situational concerns, more than what would happen. It wasn't questioning circumstances or emotions or outcomes.

It was questioning him.

Kim set the head of lettuce she'd pulled from the refrigerator down and walked over to her husband. He looked up as she fixed her dark eyes on his. She almost flinched at the hollowness she saw there, but she straightened herself tall, ready to tell the part of him she knew was saying those things to him to fuck off. She took a deep breath and opened her mouth.

"I love you."

It wasn't at all what she had expected to say, but neither her posture nor her gaze wavered.

Terry's eyes looked dull, though they stayed on hers. "I love you too." His gaze slid away then, back to the papers on the counter in front of him.

Kim let her breath out silently as Terry turned and wandered back to the living room. Reaching to straighten the pile of papers he had been examining, she returned to the counter and picked up the head of lettuce. It felt heavy in her hands.

Thanks to her internal alarm clock, Kim woke up around the time she wanted to on Saturday morning. She glanced at Terry to make sure he was still asleep and eased out of bed, tying her red satin robe around herself as she padded down the stairs.

Terry had been without a job for three weeks, and his general state seemed even more lackluster than the professional prospects he'd found. Kim was well aware that her husband's resume was exemplary – highly educated, experienced, and commended, he demonstrated unquestionable competence and even superiority in his field. The present job market was responsible for the dearth of opportunities he was finding, which made sense given that it was the reason he was unemployed in the first place.

She opened the refrigerator and grabbed two eggs, setting them on the spotless counter. All that seemed to have been forgotten by Terry. Whenever she reminded him of either his own proven competence or the obvious influence of the larger economic environment, it was as though the words dissolved in the air between them before they ever reached his powers of comprehension.

Smothering a yawn, Kim began to pull mixing bowls and measuring cups from cupboards and drawers as quietly as she could. The counter collected with ingredients as she slid canisters forward from linear rows, the immaculate surface offering itself as her canvas, a steady, solid space upon which to create. The familiar, warm appreciation for the art of food preparation spread through her body.

Picking up the griddle, she sprayed it with organic safflower oil and set it on the burner, turning the heat to low. Terry's despondence, which at this point was of more concern to her than financial matters, had been manifesting sometimes as a tightly controlled anger and bitterness and other times as a smothering despair. The night before, when he had left the kitchen after dinner with a whispered, "I'm sorry I've failed us," she had almost thrown a dish against the wall in frustration.

Kim reached for the canister of organic whole wheat flour and wiped away a spot on the side before unscrewing the lid. She reached into the container, closing her eyes and taking a deep breath as her fingers skimmed her over the softness within. She loved the feel of flour. It was one of the ingredients she most loved to touch.

It had been her conscious aim for as long as she could remember to appreciate food preparation with all of her senses. To her, cooking was nowhere near just a means to an end. It was a transformation – a miraculous process in which elements came together, often in subtly different ways, and yielded a culmination that could be substantially different from what the components had been separately. Every ingredient she used, from olive oil to molasses to a dash of salt, Kim respected as indispensable to the whole she was creating. She dismissed or took for granted none of them.

Lifting her fingers from the flour, Kim picked up a measuring cup. Her movements were reverent as she measured the ingredient precisely and transferred it to the larger mixing bowl. Then she reached for the organic brown sugar, adding the measured amount to the flour as she licked a few stray grains from her thumb. Baking soda. Two teaspoonfuls landed in white puffs on top of the dry mixture. Finally she grabbed the cinnamon, of which almost everything she baked received its ration, and tapped three brown splotches onto the powdered pile.

Her thoughts returned to her husband as she picked up the eggs. The dispiritedness Terry had displayed since losing his job had included a lack of interest in many things he usually appreciated – including sex. While she didn't take it personally, she suspected the degree to which Terry's subconscious linked his perceived professional success with his sense of basic personal value was what had made losing his job seem such like a staggering blow – and thus may seem now to be threatening his entire self-image. It wouldn't surprise her if on some level a part of him was questioning whether he was still worthy of her affection.

Kim opened the bottle of vanilla and inhaled deeply before tipping it over the bowl. She watched the thick brown ribbon swirl into the pale mixture and screwed the lid back on the small bottle. Frankly, she wasn't interested in rebuilding that particular self-image back up in Terry. The fact was, he was far more than his professional success, and while she saw nothing wrong with taking pride in it, to her Terry's reaction in the face of losing that perceived source of achievement indicated that it comprised dangerously too much of his appreciation and understanding of himself.

The griddle began to hiss, and Kim lifted the heavy bowl of pancake batter and tipped until a circle swelled on the sizzling surface. Upturning the bowl, she shifted it a few inches to start the next circle. After repeating the process twice more, she set the bowl back on the counter.

The pale circles glowed like four full moons on the black iron background as Kim began to put the ingredients away, keeping one eye on the griddle. Right after her love of cooking was her love of a clean kitchen. She aimed for her kitchen to be less than immaculate only when she was using it. Ideally, by the time whatever she was cooking was ready, the kitchen was clean again too.

Sparse bubbles began to yawn on the circles of batter like something just waking up. Kim slid the spatula under them and flipped them one by one, the bubbles receding back to the darkness of sleep. She opened a cupboard and reached toward the back. Not feeling what she wanted, she opened it further and peered inside. It took her a moment to remember they were out of syrup.

"Shit," she muttered as she shut the cupboard and tapped her fingers on the counter. She couldn't leave to run out and get some; pancakes were still cooking on the stove. Waking Terry up to do so would defeat the purpose of surprising him with breakfast in bed. She frowned.

Turning back around, she opened the cupboard again. Her eyes went to the thick, solid glass of the honey jar, honeycomb still intact in the center of the golden liquid fresh from the local apiary. Kim considered, then pulled it off the shelf and shut the cupboard door.

Unscrewing the cap, she reached across the counter for the small wooden honey drizzler and lowered it into the jar. Twirling it as she brought it back out, she watched as the barely transparent, lava-like liquid streamed back into its container. When the flow paused, Kim brought the wooden implement to her lips, opening her mouth just as the honey started to fall again. It landed on her tongue, and she moaned quietly. All the more so because of its extraordinary, unique, direct-from-nature creation process, honey was one of her favorite foods.

She turned back to the stove and pulled the pancakes from the griddle. Four more full moons were born, and Kim set the bowl down and pulled a plate from the cupboard. She dropped one of the pancakes on it and dipped the honey stick into the jar again. The amber substance spilled back into its own rippled pool as she twirled. During a pause, she moved the stick over the pancake and turned it downward, waiting as gravity slowly pulled the liquid onto the whole wheat disk below it.

Dropping the honey dipper back in the jar, Kim picked up a fork and pulled a bite toward her mouth, feeling the heat from the pancake as it got closer. She stopped short as Terry strode abruptly into view, clad in a pair of gray sweatpants.

"What are you doing?" she said, dismayed that her surprise was spoiled.

Terry rubbed his eyes sleepily. "I woke up and you weren't there. I came down to look for you." He looked behind her to the counter. "What are you doing?"

Kim glanced behind her with disappointment. "I was making you breakfast in bed."

Terry's expression registered surprise. "Oh." A smile formed across his face like the sunrise. "Thank you."

Kim smiled then too, sensing his appreciation of the unfulfilled gesture. She had planned to tell him when she woke him that she wanted to show him that they were still okay, that he was okay, that feeling like a "failure" didn't mean he wasn't worthy, that he couldn't feel happy, that he didn't deserve to be appreciated – including by himself. Most of all, to show him she loved him no matter what.

As she watched Terry, Kim saw that while her carefully executed plan had failed, the intention had been fulfilled. Though she wasn't waking her husband and telling him those things, she could see them transferring to him through the sight of the pancakes bubbling to life on the stove, the warmth of the griddle-heated air, the fragrance of cinnamon and vanilla and whole wheat surrounding them. She hadn't needed to say a word.

"I forgot we were out of syrup." Kim moved back to the counter and flipped the pancakes on the griddle before lifting the honey jar. "I was just checking to see how they tasted with honey." A drop had fallen onto the counter, a single slip of disorder among meticulousness.

Terry's mouth curved in a smile as he followed her. "A spot on the counter!" he teased, pointing at it. Kim smirked and grabbed a kitchen wipe to clean it up. Terry laughed, and Kim spun around and looked into his eyes. It was a magical sound – one she hadn't heard in weeks.

Her husband pulled the honey jar from her. Kim watched as he lifted the drizzler out slowly, his eyes on the golden liquid as it spiraled back into the pool in the jar. He motioned with his head for her to come closer. Kim started to question, but before she could speak he closed the distance between them himself and untied her robe so swiftly it fell to the ground before she could grab it. He flicked the burner off behind her as he nudged her back against the counter and lifted the honey drizzler to her neck.

Kim started to protest as the amber liquid began to drip, but she froze as it touched her skin. She squirmed as a drop fell to the floor, but Terry pushed on her shoulder, holding her against the counter. She started to speak again, and the words dissipated as he pressed his mouth to the honey flowing like lava over her clavicle. His warm tongue swept over her skin as he claimed the sweet liquid from it.

"Terry," Kim managed to admonish when he pulled away. She gasped as honey landed on her breast – she hadn't noticed his hand moving back to the jar. As she watched, openmouthed, Terry glided the dipper several inches above her chest, drizzling honey in a horizontal line across her breasts.

The sticky liquid began to descend, creeping toward her nipples. Kim opened her mouth to object as Terry dipped his head and caught a nipple between his teeth just as it was engulfed. Her breath caught in her throat, and she remained silent as he grasped her breast from underneath, his tongue swirling over the golden sweetness.

Terry groped her other breast with his other hand, smearing honey across her skin as she let out a muffled moan. He followed it with his mouth, fervently licking the mess he had just made and grabbing the breast his mouth had just left. His mouth and hands became a flurry of action, emphasized all the more by the slowness of the honey as it inched along her skin. Kim lost track of where Terry's hands were and where honey would next land on her body as he lifted her to sit on the counter, his tongue roving her breasts, her nipples, her neck, her throat, her stomach.

She gasped when she felt the distinct sensation of the liquid dropping onto her lower belly and beginning to slide downward. Terry grasped her thighs and pushed them further apart as he hovered, waiting as the honey traveled down her skin. Kim's breath was suspended, barely moving as her cunt pulsed, nothing but the anticipation of Terry's mouth landing there holding any more of her attention. She glanced down to where the liquid shone like glass on her dark skin, moving like a melting glacier toward the heat that awaited it.

The moment the cascade reached her clit, Terry dove. Kim inhaled sharply and dropped her head back, digging her fingers into her husband's hair as he licked and sucked, thoroughly collecting all honey from her clitoris.

To her surprise, Kim felt a climax building as his tongue quivered against her. Orgasm had not usually happened so quickly for her, but now, seconds after Terry's first contact with her clit, it felt imminent.

Panting, she dropped back on her elbows. Just as the wave was about to come, Terry rose, scooping her off the counter and setting her onto the honey-dotted floor in one swift motion. Kim's resistance to the messiness of the usually impeccable linoleum subsided as his mouth returned to its previous position. Terry grabbed her ankles and threw them over his shoulders as he squeezed at her tits, his tongue never ceasing its work.

Heat roiled in her like water in a teakettle. When she reached the boiling point she screeched in kind, flailing wildly as the orgasm ravished her honey-drenched body. She rolled in the stickiness, utter and inexplicable surrender making her not just ignore but revel in the messiness, the chaos, the letting go of something she hadn't even known she was holding on to. Her body seemed to sink deeper into the puddles of honey beneath it as Terry's hands gripped her thighs firmly, all traces of the amber liquid long gone from the surface of her clit, still covered by his mouth.

She breathed heavily, opening her eyes, and looked up at her husband. The same embrace of chaos, disorder, upheaval was reflected in his gaze as he looked back at her, love enveloping the two of them like the honey that covered her body as she reached for him.

Uncertainty. Messiness. Surrender. They were part of the recipe. Something had moved, and it went beyond what she had wanted Terry to understand a few hours before when she'd trotted purposefully down the steps in her short crimson robe. Because it had moved in her too. Like the alchemy in cooking, something had been created in the connection, the collaboration, that was greater than and different from the components by themselves.

The kitchen wasn't clean. But it was what it needed to be to have created what was there. Terry's mouth found hers, and Kim tasted honey as he kissed her. She wrapped herself around him, their bodies at ease as they lay immersed in the sticky disarray.

The Plant on the Mantel

Sylvia stepped in front of me into the large living room of the house her grandparents had inhabited. The room itself was like one large shadow. The night outside the windows draped the walls, carpet, furniture, even the very air with its mystery.

Though the house was only an hour and a half from where we lived, it was my first time here. Sylvia's grandfather had died right before we got married – her grandmother had died years before – and since then Sylvia's aunt Jolene had moved in temporarily to keep the house in the family. Now Jolene was relocating, and the decision had been made to sell it. For the next few weeks the family would be combing through the things left in it, making sure all was accounted for and claimed or donated.

Sylvia walked to the front of the room where the majestic fireplace rose five feet from the ground, the mantel over it resting at about eye level. She stopped in front of it.

"That plant is generations old," she said. "My mother told me she remembers its being around for as long as she can remember."

"No kidding," I said, joining her in front of the fireplace.

"It's a wax plant. She was told it was there for years before she was born."

The plant itself was full and long, its numerous appendages draping across the mantle and running down the side of the fireplace to brush the floor. It reigned on the outermost corner of the mantle, higher than anything else on that surface, its leaves appearing a dark green gloss in the almost absent light. I wondered about its needing sun, then realized the mantle was only a few yards from the tall east-facing window to the left, which would offer unchecked access to morning sunlight.

I looked more closely at the thick stems. They twirled and twisted, climbing like ivy and draping like linen across the mantle and down the side of the wrought-iron fireplace cage. Two of its tentacles had spiraled around the black iron, as though casually marking its territory in this, its unquestioned place in the home.

"That means this plant witnessed your mother's whole life here – as well as much of your grandparents'," I said.

Sylvia had turned to her left and was looking at the large portrait in the middle of the wall with the windows. Her back was to me as she nodded silently.

"My grandmother had an affair," she said abruptly, staring at the portrait.

My eyebrows rose. "Really?"

She nodded. "It was brief. When my mother was very young."

"I had no idea."

"Neither did we. We didn't find out until we were going through her things after the funeral and found some old letters."

I stared at the portrait, the calm, majestic-looking woman with a bit of a smile on her face, holding secrets even her family didn't know until her death.

Sylvia turned back to the fireplace and stepped forward, running her fingers over the thick leaves of the wax plant. "I hadn't thought about those letters for a long time."

"Heh. I guess that plant could have seen even more than I was thinking," I joked.

Sylvia ran her gaze up and down it, fingertips still grazing the shiny leaves as they reflected the starlight from the window. She did not laugh, but finally answered in a faraway voice, "Yes. It could have."

I entered the bedroom as Sylvia was turning down the sheets, already in her nightgown. Her countenance was thoughtful, as it had been since our return from her grandparents' estate.

"What's going to happen to the plant?" I asked her.

"What?" She straightened and turned to me.

"The plant. At your grandparents' house. Where's it going to go?"

"Oh," her voice sounded casual, but for some reason I suspected the thought wasn't new to her. She paused. "I don't know."

"It just seems kind of important, it being so old. Seems like someone should take care of it."

Sylvia looked introspective and nodded.

"I never really knew my grandmother," she said after a silence.

I looked at her, unsure where this new thread was going.

"I mean, we lived much further away from them when I was growing up, and I was only 19 when she died." Sylvia sat on the bed, still not looking at me.

"Her affair seemed... mysterious. I wonder if there are more letters that we didn't find, or how it ended, or why. I wonder if my grandfather found out. My mom and sister and I found the letters – we decided not to mention them to him," she added.

I had wondered those things briefly too, but since she hadn't volunteered any information, I hadn't wanted to ask. I watched her. She still hadn't looked at me.

"They were very... explicit. The letters, I mean." I thought I saw Sylvia blush faintly, and a soft, spontaneous smile lifted my lips.

She looked at me then and saw it. "Yeah, I know, you think I'm a prude," she said with a self-deprecating smile, huffing a little as she looked back down.

I went to the bed and sat beside her. "No, I don't think you're a 'prude,'" I said. I didn't. She tended to be somewhat reserved verbally and publicly about sex, but it didn't stop her from letting loose when it came down to the act. I smiled. "I just think it's interesting that you would seem surprised that your grandmother may have been sexually 'explicit.'"

Sylvia blushed more and laughed a little, still looking down. "Well, it's admittedly not something I ever thought about in relation to her. I just experienced my grandparents as so... stiff. You know?"

I shrugged. "Maybe that's why she did it. Maybe she didn't fit in with that environment and needed more than she was getting."

Sylvia looked up at me, slight surprise in her expression.

"I'm sorry," I said immediately. "I didn't mean to be disrespectful to your grandfather." I paused. "I almost forgot who we were talking about for a minute."

She looked back down, nodding. "Yeah. I know what you mean. That happened to me earlier this evening when you talked about the plant. What it had seen." Her voice trailed off. "It's weird to think that it was sitting there that whole time, all those years, in that same place. It's been alive and sitting on that mantle for more than half a century."

I pictured the motionless collection of sturdy leaves, twined together and looped around each other and the surrounding objects, growing languidly for six decades in the best seat in the room for anything that took place there.

"In the letters, they talked about being in that room," Sylvia said.

"Really?"

She nodded. "There was one where – " she stopped and blushed, and I felt myself smile again. Sylvia had talked about sex in a communicative context, if not exactly technical then informative, when we had discussed various matters between us. I hadn't usually perceived her as shy. But it was true that she had rarely talked about sex just for the sake of talking about it, spoken explicitly for anything other than practical purposes. Done it for the pure pleasure or underlying naughtiness of it.

Was that what she was doing now?

"Never mind," she said with a little giggle. "Why am I going on about this?"

I grabbed her hand as she started to stand. She looked down at it, then at me, with surprise.

"I'd like to hear about it," I said quietly, looking in her eyes. "I'd like to hear what you were going to say."

Sylvia stared at me, motionless, then slowly sat back down beside me.

I turned to face her. "Tell me what the letter said," I invited.

She blushed again and looked down, but I could tell she was going to continue this time.

"It was from her to him. I read it when I was alone one day, going through things in their office. We'd already found the box of letters, but no one else had taken much interest in them."

She took a deep breath. "It talked about being in that room. It even mentioned the plant, actually." She gave a tiny laugh and glanced up to meet my eyes before dropping them again. "It said... she was talking about coming back in from a horseback ride they took together. My grandfather was away for a few days. She talked about how he..."

As I listened to her voice and saw amidst her hesitation a hint of arousal, I started to get hard. This had turned her on. There was no question. She wouldn't be so shy about relating it now if she hadn't felt turned on by the letter. I watched her pink cheeks and subtly deeper breathing and felt the urge to climb on top of her. I exhaled slowly and tempered it, waiting for her to finish telling the story she wanted to tell.

"It mentioned the sex they had had on a blanket in the field while the horses were resting," she almost whispered, and at that moment, attempting to picture such a thing, I could understand Sylvia's surprise.

"And how when they got back to the house, she went to bathe while he stayed in the living room, and when she came in she was wearing only her slip. And he had turned to her and been so shocked but so turned on that he had thrown her down on the couch and taken her there. That's how she put it – she said 'threw me down on the couch.' Obviously she liked it though," she added quickly.

"And when they were done she got up, and she stayed naked. She talked about how it was the first time she'd done that, that she'd never walked around naked in front of someone, even her husband." Sylvia fell quiet for a moment. "I got the impression – that was important to her somehow."

I nodded. Simply hearing it this way from Sylvia, I had that feeling too.

Sylvia smiled, then chuckled. "Then she said she went and got the watering can to water 'the plant on the mantel,'" she said with a laugh. "Naked! She's reminiscing about it being one of the things she did naked after they'd had sex on the couch."

I smiled at Sylvia. She stopped laughing as she met my gaze, her expression falling into a soft smile. I leaned forward and caught the back of her neck in my hand, my mouth falling on hers. I slid my tongue into it and heard her catch her breath as I felt her seamless response against my lips. She was as turned on as I was, I realized, and I pushed her back against the pillows as her breathing deepened and her arms came around me.

I was fully hard. I reached down and pulled at her nightgown, wanting it out of the way as she grabbed my pants and pulled them open with the same urgency. Wanting inside her so badly it hurt, I sank into her the moment our clothes were yanked away and discarded.

Sylvia moaned in a way she usually didn't until she was close to orgasm. Her body pushed into mine, making me feel breathless and heated in a way I hadn't in some time.

So much so that I began an unexpected monologue in her ear.

"What else do you think the plant on the mantle saw?" I whispered roughly, exertion and arousal seeming to push the words out of me. "How many times do you think they fucked in that room? How many times did he shove his hand up her skirt, did she rip the corset from her body feeling just like you do now, wanting that cock hard inside her, taking her. How many times did he bend her over the back of the couch, rubbing her clit from behind? Did they fuck again that day after she walked around naked? Did she sit him down, stand in front of him in all her undressed glory as he watched, reclaiming something that had always been hers but somehow been denied for so long?"

I didn't even know what I was saying; the words were simply coming out of me as I pumped into Sylvia. She gasped in my ear, crying out occasionally. The words seemed to be searing into her too, pooling the wetness I could feel around my cock, and as I came I cried out, my pace increasing to a frenzy as the climax erupted from my entire body.

I lay on top of her, breathing heavily, as she continued to move beneath me. I knew she was close, and I slid out of her and snaked my hand between our bodies and her legs, brushing my finger over her clit. Her intake of breath was sharp, and I circled my fingers gently, then harder as I sensed that was what she needed. In moments she began to shudder, wailing without restraint as her body thrashed beneath my hand. Her eyes were closed.

As she worked to catch her breath, she opened them and turned to me. Speaking suddenly felt alien, and there was nothing but a thick, panting silence between us as our eyes held each other's, words, which had served such an intense purpose only moments before, now content to lie still for a while, gazing silently upon the results of their work.

After a while Sylvia reached up and ran her hand along my cheek. With a lazy smile she whispered, "We'll go pick up the plant first thing tomorrow."

Relative Anonymity

She and David had married young. They'd known each other all their lives – their parents had been good friends since high school – and at the time, it seemed the thing to do. So at the tender age of 20, they were married in the town's small Baptist church surrounded by the people they'd known all their lives.

They lived happily enough for seven years on their own farm two miles from her parents', three miles from his. It was beautiful and charming and calm, the routine of the farm as steady and predictable as the rise and set of the sun that marked their workdays.

Carly wasn't sure when she started to realize it, and she wasn't sure when David did either. But she remembered the day the two of them stood in the kitchen, when their gazes had locked and they knew: they loved each other – just not as husband and wife. The same connection that had been between them as long as they could remember, that had allowed them to know each other more intimately than anyone else, allowed them to see with undeniable clarity what they both knew the moment their eyes met that day. Tears had fallen from both pairs as they'd moved into a silent embrace.

The divorce was as quiet and intimate as their tiny country wedding had been. David had chosen to stay on the farm in their rural Nebraska town and live in their house. Carly wasn't sure how she knew leaving was the right thing for her to do, but she did.

Sometimes looking at her life had felt like looking at scenes from a book; they fit together perfectly, but she almost hadn't felt inside or a part of them. She and David grew up together, their families were best friends, and they loved each other, but their marriage was like a piece of a puzzle of overall togetherness that the situation required. "They as a couple" had sometimes seemed like no more than a congeniality, a formality to complete things the way they were supposed to be completed. Was it about privacy? Maybe. Carly wasn't even sure what she meant by that, but she knew that privacy had seemed like a mysterious, elusive concept that occurred in other people's lives.

So she left. Nebraska held everything in life that she loved; yet she felt there was nothing there left for her. She'd moved more than a thousand miles away, to the East coast, entering city life for the first time. She had been back home to visit at least twice every year since she'd left, and she and David kept in touch.

When David had called three weeks before and said there was something he wanted to talk to her about, she had invited him to go ahead. He said he wanted to tell her in person – that it wasn't urgent, but he was wondering when she next planned to visit.

Carly had guessed David was seeing someone, that it was getting serious, and that he wanted them to meet. She'd smiled softly as a pang of nostalgia pulled her heart. She could understand his desire, and since she hadn't been back since Christmas and had always enjoyed the early-summer atmosphere of her rural hometown, she'd checked her schedule and booked a flight.

The farm looked precisely as she remembered it. She had seen David since the divorce, but always gathered at his or her parents' house or somewhere as part of a get-together. This was the first time she had returned to the home they had shared for seven years.

She slammed the car door and squinted at the ordered rows of corn that stretched far from the yard to her left. The field was the view from the kitchen window inside, and Carly remembered the countless times she'd stood there and seen David harvesting, the red combine gliding and turning like a tiny windup toy on the far side of the field.

The screen door squeaked open, and Carly turned. David stood framed. He smiled and waved, and she waved back before heading up the driveway to the yard.

She met his eyes as she did. He looked great, but there was something different in his eyes. Though she couldn't tell what it was, it was definitely there. They looked darker, deeper, less like the straight blue gaze she had always known and more like something more solemn now lay behind it.

Settled with iced tea at the kitchen table, Carly leaned back and rested her feet on the rung of the chair beside her. There had been no indication of anyone else around, and she began to wonder if her suspicion had been erroneous.

"I'm moving away," David said.

Carly looked at him in surprise. "Away from here?"

He nodded. He appeared calm, fairly unmoved by the idea, which surprised her. But as she looked at him, she understood suddenly that he was feeling the exact same way she had when she had left three years before.

"Well wow. I had no idea. No one said anything to me about it, amazingly enough. When?"

"They don't know." David looked at her. Peace, she noticed with a start. That was the depth in his eyes. Carly felt surprise in that she had never thought of David as not at peace before, but the impression, though understated, was distinct.

"They don't know you're leaving?" Carly guessed he was referring to their respective families and other acquaintances in this small town – which was virtually everyone.

David shook his head. "I'll be asking Dan to take over the farm, which I'm pretty sure won't be a problem."

Carly nodded. She wanted to ask how his brother was doing, but she sensed David had more to say.

David tipped back his glass and stretched his long, jeans-clad legs out in front of him. There was silence for several minutes as his gaze rested on his cowboy boots.

"I need to ask you to keep this in confidence, Carly. And I really mean that," he said, turning his head to meet her gaze.

A bit taken aback, she said, "Sure."

"I trust you, that's why it feels okay to me to tell you this, but I'm serious."

Carly stared at him. She had no qualms about keeping a secret, and she understood how much of a challenge that was in a small town. His trust in her was not misplaced, but she couldn't fathom what he had to say to her.

David stood and motioned her to follow.

He led her down to the basement, where their old farming tools, extra and reject horse equipment, and other farm paraphernalia were stored. The basement was mostly unfinished, but its existence had been important to them – tornadoes were not taken lightly in this part of the country.

Carly walked behind him down the steep staircase in the dark, glancing ahead to the shadows on the concrete floor. She narrowed her eyes at a large shape she didn't recognize as they reached the bottom.

David turned on the light. Carly blinked.

The basement no longer held farm equipment. At least, not in sight.

She looked around, keeping her expression neutral, though not without effort. The shape she had seen was a cross, life-size, with attached wrist and ankle cuffs dangling from it. Carly wasn't entirely sheltered enough to not know what it was for, but she had never seen one in person. Beyond the cross was a sawhorse that looked ready for its traditional purpose except for the black padding across the top and leather cuffs identical to the ones on the cross attached to each of the four legs.

Her eyes went to the trunk against the wall that used to hold old horse-grooming equipment. It didn't anymore. It was open, and Carly saw things that were becoming less surprising: whips, floggers, paddles, and a number of contraptions she wasn't sure she knew how to label or identify.

Carly cleared her throat. "Did you have a yard sale with the horse and farm equipment?"

David smiled. "Thanks for not freaking out," he said quietly. His voice rose to normal volume. "All the old equipment and storage is in the back room." He nodded toward the dark doorway to the room Carly imagined was rather crowded now. David's eyes roved around. "I... redecorated."

"Yes..."

David moved forward and ran his hand along the cross, his fingertips brushing the silver hardware of a wrist cuff. Carly was about to say more when a knock on the basement door that led outside made her jump.

"Come in." David raised his voice just enough to be heard outside the door. Carly looked at him. She didn't ever remember their using that door.

The door opened slowly. Carly's view was blocked by it, but from where he stood David had a clear view of who was behind it.

"Hi sweetheart," he said. "Thanks for coming."

Carly blushed. He was bringing a woman in there while she was there? Did he think he had to show her how this stuff was used? Did he think she was interested?

The heat intensified in her face. Was she interested?

Watching David with another woman certainly wasn't something it had occurred to her she wanted to see when she came there, but an unexpected intrigue and a bit of arousal shot through her.

The door opened further, and the one David had called "sweetheart" stepped into view. Carly stared.

The man was about six feet tall. He wore jeans, a white button-down shirt, and battered brown cowboy boots. He was about ten years younger than they were, and very good-looking.

And he was the town preacher's son.

"Hi, Carly," he said quietly, glancing at the floor.

It took Carly a second to find her voice. When she did, she shook herself.

"Hello, Nate," she said, stepping forward to shake his hand. He appeared ill at ease, and despite her shock, Carly didn't want him to feel uncomfortable. She smiled, albeit somewhat dazedly, and lifted her other hand to join it with the one already holding his. "How are you?"

Nate met her eyes and acknowledged the question with a nod. "Okay. You?"

Carly nodded. "I'm fine."

"So, it's probably obvious what I wanted to tell you," David cut in at her side.

Moving away, bondage, men... any of the three would have surprised her about David. To have them come in a cluster was something she had a feeling might not even hit her full force until later.

"How long has this been going on?" she asked.

"Four months."

Carly nodded slowly. "Impressive that you haven't been found out yet."

"Yes. I would rather not be, obviously. But for Nate..." Nate looked up and gave them a tight smile before dropping his eyes back to the floor. David didn't have to continue – he didn't have to explain how much Nate didn't want to be caught. "Nate's been helping out at the farm, so there's been an excuse for his being here."

Carly nodded. That would be helpful, yes.

"So I wondered if you'd like to see it," David said.

"See it?" Carly echoed. She wondered if she understood what he meant.

"See what we do."

David kept his gaze on her, and she didn't answer. Without a word he gestured to the love seat behind her, inviting her to sit. Carly backed the few steps without breaking eye contact and lowered herself to the edge of the love seat.

David turned back to Nate. Within seconds they were kissing, and Carly felt herself blush from the obvious heat between them. Like an abstract screen saver, clothing gave way and turned to skin before her eyes, and soon they were half-naked before her, still standing, hands roaming like eels curling through water. Carly realized her lips were parted and closed them, glancing prudently at the floor.

The rest of Nate's clothes came off, and David, wearing only his jeans and boots, led him to the cross. He lifted Nate's strong arms and secured them into the wrist cuffs one at a time, and Carly caught her breath at the view of Nate's considerable biceps displayed below his bound wrists. The vision captivated her, actually, and Carly found herself almost panting as she stared, her eyes running eventually from the arms down the strong torso to the unambiguous hard-on protruding from Nate's body. Nate was in slightly better shape than David, which wasn't surprising given his age and the manual labor he did daily on the farm. David's body had looked similar a decade ago.

After fastening the ankle cuffs, David stood and ran his fingertips lightly up the underside of Nate's cock. Carly heard the younger man's breath change, but he made no movement save the involuntary flutter of his jaw muscle and slight drooping of his already hooded eyelids.

David backed up and went to the trunk. Pulling out a flogger, he ran it lightly up Nate's cock, the fringes sliding over the latter's erection with the gentleness of dandelion seeds blowing in the wind. Nate's face muscles twitched, his breath shifting to a pant.

Carly watched, mesmerized.

Abruptly David pulled his arm back and slapped Nate across the chest with the flogger. Carly blinked in surprise. Nate winced, and his hard-on seemed to surge forward and up.

David slashed the flogger across Nate's rigid cock, and Carly almost winced. As she watched, David worked the flogger all around Nate's body before backing up and lifting from the trunk a narrow cane. The crack against Nate's skin this time did make Carly cringe, and she watched closely, unable to imagine how Nate could be enjoying what was happening.

But from the rampant rigidity of his cock, he seemed to be.

After a brief bout with the cane, David reached and unbuckled the silver hardware of the wrist cuffs holding Nate in place. He trailed his fingertips down his lover's chest as he bent to undo the ankle cuffs. Despite the welts now covering his skin, Nate showed no reaction beyond his heavy breathing.

David gestured with his head, and the young man draped his body over the nearby sawhorse. David latched all four cuffs in place and stood in front of his partner.

Then he stepped back and unzipped his pants. Nate's head extended like a turtle's from a shell, reaching for the cock millimeters from his mouth. David touched his lips with it and then stood back, leaning forward occasionally to brush it against the younger man's skin.

Carly, entranced, suddenly realized she was looking at the cock of the man who used to be her husband. The cock that had been inside her countless times, that she had seen on a regular basis for almost a decade. It now hovered in front of another man's mouth, one it was a safe bet it had been in before. Carly felt something stir in her, but she wasn't sure what it was.

She wasn't sure what she felt at all.

Abruptly David shoved his cock forward with such force Carly was startled, and she almost gasped as Nate's mouth opened automatically to take it. David thrust forward rhythmically, gripping Nate's hair as he slammed his cock deep into his throat. Carly couldn't see the evidence of Nate's arousal now, but she guessed from his muffled moans that it had changed little.

David yanked his cock away and took a step back, and Carly could feel the hunger emanating from Nate as his head lowered. It was a hunger that she, as one who loved to suck cock herself, understood.

David moved around behind the sawhorse, never glancing Carly's way. Neither of them had looked at her since the introduction had been made, and she wondered if they remembered she was there. She had a sense that the intensity in front of her was so acute it may leave no room to recall anything else. She certainly didn't have a feeling they were putting on a show.

David had procured a condom and rolled it down his rock-hard dick. Standing behind Nate, who was still breathing heavily but otherwise completely still, he poured lube into his hand and ran it up his cock slowly, his slick fist sliding easily up and down the rubber. With his clean hand, he reached and palmed one of Nate's buttocks. Then he drew back and slapped hard, murmuring something Carly couldn't quite make out as Nate whimpered. The slapping and low monologue continued, words she couldn't hear but a tone that she could. A combination of taunting and reassurance, simultaneously warm and ominous. She wondered what David was saying and strained her ears as he delivered one final smack and pushed his way into Nate's ass.

David's buttocks flexed and dented as he shoved his cock in and out of Nate, the latter helplessly bound to the sawhorse as he grunted, sweat showing now on his forehead. Carly watched with unabashed fascination, alternating between incredulity at her voyeuristic position and the surreal awareness that she was watching someone she had been married to and known all her life.

And something else had emerged in her too. Carly crossed her legs and shifted a bit as David pounded away at his submissive. She wasn't attracted to David personally anymore, but it felt impossible not to be aroused by the simple carnal attraction exploding before her eyes. Her ex-husband grunted as he slammed into Nate, involuntary sounds emanating from Nate's throat as he took David's sizable cock. David fucked him with no apparent restraint, occasionally smacking the younger man's ass.

David leaned forward and grabbed his partner by the hair, yanking his head up and back as Nate let out a groan. David pumped more frenetically, tangling both hands in Nate's hair as he came with a roar.

Carly was breathless, her chest moving perceptibly as she pulled air in through her mouth. She did not remember when her mouth had fallen open, or when her breath had turned to gasps. Her panting, though silent, mirrored David's as he backed away from Nate. She watched as he disposed of the condom and attended to undoing the restraints holding Nate's wrists. She wondered if they were done.

They were not.

In hindsight, Carly realized she should have known that. David had never been an inconsiderate lover. There might be an obvious power play going on, but she saw shortly that it didn't mean anyone was denied what he was obviously there for.

Nate followed David back to the cross, where David re-cuffed him facing forward again. If it was possible, Carly noticed Nate's cock seemed even harder than it had before, appearing almost painfully purple and, she could only imagine, needing release. She wondered in what form it would come.

David leaned in and gripped Nate's throat, hissing low in his ear. Knowing she wouldn't be able to hear what was said, Carly just watched. David ran his fingers slowly over Nate's engorged cock as he murmured, his tone switching back to the gentle taunting she had heard him use earlier.

Nate winced at the contact of David's fingers, and Carly wondered if it didn't feel more torturous than all of the beating Nate had endured so far.

David's voice seemed to rise in a question, and a breathless Nate nodded in desperation, as though his head was acting of its own accord to agree to whatever would result in his being allowed to come. The cock on which David's hand still rested seemed like a volcano ready to blow.

He let go of it and backed up, looking straight at Nate. When David turned his head to look at her, Carly jumped. His eye contact was like a sudden burn, the intensity of the scene reflected in – or perhaps emanating from – his eyes seeming to transfer straight to her with his gaze.

He smiled. She smiled back, baffled.

Raising his eyebrows, he gestured with his hand at Nathan's cock. It appeared to be an invitation. Carly blinked, her eyes widening.

There was a pause, and David said evenly, "Would you like to finish him off, Carly?"

Her mouth dropped open again, though this time she was aware of it. She looked at Nate, who continued to stare straight ahead, still breathless, his cock painfully swollen. Carly realized she felt no hesitation in wanting – she did indeed want to make that cock blow.

What was the hesitation, then? She looked back at David, who still held her gaze, his expression open and inviting as though he had just offered to get her a drink at a party. The whole of their lives together seemed to flash through her imagination: chasing each other as kids through the edges of the cornfields, playing on hay bales in the barn until the sun went down and they were called inside, making out behind the grain bins at the back of his family's farm in high school, riding the horses out night after night the summer after they graduated to the deserted plot of land her family owned. Farming and living and working and sleeping side by side for seven years in the house where she now stood, after they had been married by the father of the man shackled to the cross a few feet away.

And now here they were. Back in the same house, the man who had been her husband inviting her to suck another man's cock.

His lover's.

Carly stared into David's blue eyes, remembering the day they had looked at each other and faced what they both knew and both knew the other knew: they didn't want to be married to each other. There was something else out there for both of them.

Carly blinked and broke her gaze. For David, that certainly seemed to be the case.

She looked back at him, and he smiled a smile that was so familiar she almost gasped. At that moment she would have sworn he had just seen the same movie of their lives together she had, some connection even now in the look between them allowing them to share the same memory.

She took a step forward. David backed up to allow her through, his hand gallantly brushing her lower back as she stepped to the cross.

Nate's breath was even now, though sweat was still gathered on his face. His eyes were downcast, and Carly stood in front of him until he raised his eyes to hers. She didn't know him well enough to read them, but she saw nothing to indicate fear or resistance to what she was about to do, which was what she was checking for. She trusted David, but she was in undeniably unfamiliar territory, and she didn't want to be a pawn in a power game of which Nate was unwitting.

She should have known better.

Nate gasped sharply as she knelt and touched her lips to his cock. She had planned to go slowly, to tease a little bit, but the obvious hunger of the cock in front of her combined with the arousal in her she hadn't known the degree of until that moment propelled her forward without restraint, and she sucked Nate's cock with the same vigor and aggression with which David had fucked his ass.

Predictably, the young man came in seconds, the vocal accompaniment sounding both the desperation and the euphoria of the release. He spurted into her mouth repeatedly as she kept sucking, letting his warm come run out of her lips and down her chin as she took his cock all the way to the back of her throat and felt it continue to shoot there. Eventually she pulled back, her mouth, lips, and face a warm, sticky mess. She glanced up at the man shackled to the cross. His eyes were closed, his head thrown back. His body hung limply, as though the restraints now held him up.

Carly backed up on her knees and stood, wiping her mouth with the back of her hand. Her heart was still pounding, her knees slightly shaky as she backed out of the way to give David room to undo Nate's bindings. The charge was such that she had almost come herself, and she imagined it wouldn't take much to do so once she was back in her car alone with her fingers. Her climax would come, she suspected, before she reached the end of the driveway.

"I wanted you to see it. See it that way," David said. His voice was low, and Carly remembered the rumbling sound of it when he had spoken to Nate and she hadn't been able to hear what he'd said. She nodded.

"I didn't know what you'd say, what you'd think. I didn't know how to tell you. I felt like there was no way to tell you." His blue eyes pierced into hers. He shrugged. "So I thought I'd show you."

Carly nodded again. The conversation they were having almost seemed more surreal than the experience itself, as it was devoid of the adrenaline charges of sexual arousal and surprise. She was left having what would seem a mundane conversation with her ex-husband, intermittent with flashbacks in her imagination of the scene they had undergone the day before.

"I understand." She paused. "I'm curious, though – did you plan to... have me...?"

David shook his head. "No, I didn't plan on your being involved." He shrugged again, giving her a rakish smile. "I just went with my instinct. They haven't seemed wrong yet when it's come to you."

Carly smiled and dropped her eyes. It was quiet for a few moments as she studied the floor.

"Well, I'd better get going. My flight leaves in a few hours." Carly stood up. She paused and looked back down at David, recalling why he had called her there in the first place. "You said you're leaving. Are the two of you leaving together?" She didn't say, but it seemed to her such evidence would be almost as damning in this small town as it would if they were discovered here.

He shook his head. "No. I'm going first. I'll be taking off in about three weeks. I'm going to the Omaha area – I wrote the address for you to take with you on the counter." David nodded at a sheet of paper there. "Nate's going to wait until the end of the summer. He's going to go to grad school at the University of Nebraska there. We're not going to live together right now. We'd still be too easily found out that way." David shrugged. "I don't know what will happen, to tell you the truth. I've been thinking about getting out of here for some time, though. Nate's wanted to for years."

"Would... would his parents finding out have the implications I imagine for Nate?"

"Yes." The answer came before the sentence was finished.

Carly lowered her head. She felt tears forming and took a deep breath. "I wish you both the best," she said sincerely, stepping forward as David stood to meet her in a hug.

"I know," David whispered near her ear. "That's why I told you."

Carly fingered the slip of paper with David's soon-to-be address on it as she stared out the airplane window. It was funny. She had lamented the seeming lack of privacy in their lives, their relationship, while they were married. The complete support from their families was not only unquestioned but at times felt to her too much so. She couldn't imagine what the ominous specter of so much the opposite felt like to David now. And even more so to Nate.

How long would they wait? What if they were found out? Would they come out themselves? Did they really want to leave – or did they feel like they had to? Carly watched the green and yellow patchwork of Midwest fields shrink below her, feeling like what she had learned almost seemed to spawn more questions than it answered.

But maybe they weren't for her to have answered. Or maybe they were part of something everyone had to answer, innumerable questions that took different forms but were ultimately all the same. Questions asked of everyone, including not only David and Nate but also Nate's father, her parents, David's parents, every resident of the tiny Nebraska town she had just left, and everyone who lived in the city toward which she now headed. And herself.

Carly glanced at the paper in her hand. She was returning to a place where she had relative anonymity, a luxury neither David nor Nate had – yet. Her eyes scanned the unfamiliar address written in familiar handwriting. She folded the paper and leaned forward to slip it into her purse, then settled back, watching the receding fields below fade from sight.

Maybe they were questions that didn't have answers. Questions that somehow, by the very asking, allowed life itself.

Shattered Angels

Shelley shivered as she took off her coat and hung it on the hook behind her office door. The fall wind was biting. Unwinding her scarf, she walked around the desk and picked up the two file folders on her chair, deducing they were the two new case applications Gary had let her know she would be receiving. As she dropped them on her desk and sat down, the phone rang.

"Hi, baby, it's me," her husband said when she answered it. "I was just checking the weather in Niagara Falls for this weekend, and it looks like it's supposed to rain at least part of the time we're there. I wanted to let you know while I was thinking about it so you could pack accordingly."

Shelley held back a smile as she pulled the file from the visitation she'd just finished from her briefcase. "Gee, thanks, Kenny. That was so important that it just couldn't wait until we were at home – which, of course, is where I will be doing said packing?"

"Hey, I just wanted to let you know."

Shelley laughed. She knew he was excited. And she was too. Despite everything, Niagara Falls remained one of her favorite places.

"Your diligent concentration on work is inspiring," she teased him.

"I put my organizational skills to use preemptively scheduling so I don't have to get a damn thing done this week. Anyway, I just wanted to check in. I'd better get back to not working now."

Shelley chuckled as she hung up the phone. The trip to Niagara Falls was their five-year wedding anniversary present to each other. It had been the runner-up choice for their honeymoon destination, edged out by the exotic lure of Greece, and they had made a pact at the time to go to Niagara Falls to celebrate their fifth anniversary.

Though her family had taken several trips to the Falls when she and Nikki were kids, it had been years since Shelley had been there. She twirled in her chair and looked out the window, her smile fading. As usual, her eyes went to the church across the street. A huge, dark gray structure, it was a sprawling vision of silence and stability in this rough and parlous neighborhood. Her third-floor window at the youth center was at eye level with the spires that towered above three giant stained-glass panes that were the obvious centerpiece of the building's facade.

The glow of colored glass held her attention until Shelley bit her lip and turned around, determined to pull herself away from painful memories before they began. Still, despite herself, she quickly pulled up the Niagara Falls tourism site to check Kenny's report before she delved into the two new folders on her desk. The mouse clicked away beneath her thumb as she followed the familiar links to get to the weather page.

She smiled wryly at the little raincloud icon beneath the date two days away before automatically glancing at the animated advertisement in the right sidebar. She froze at the sight of the monarch that flitted away into the digital ether to be replaced by a message advertising the Butterfly Conservatory at Niagara Falls. Shelley stared at the screen, unable to pull her gaze from the cheerful looping ad.

Nikki had loved butterflies. Her sister's highlight of the family's first trip to the Falls, when Nikki was eleven and Shelley eight, had clearly been their visit to see the butterflies in the sprawling, plant-filled glass enclosure advertised on the screen in front of Shelley right now. They'd seemed to like her too, landing on Nikki constantly, flicking against her skin or roosting on the sleeve of her shirt to the fascination of the other visitors. Shelley, wanting them to land on her, too, had followed her older sister, earnestly holding out her fingers to the creatures flitting among tropical flowers around them. But nary a one had shown interest in her, even as they flocked around Nikki as though she were some kind of butterfly whisperer.

At the time, Shelley had been jealous. Now there wasn't much she wouldn't give to see her sister with butterflies dancing around her, smiling with the grace of someone truly enchanted by them.

Miniature angels. That's what Nikki had called them, comparing their wings to the stained glass that graced the cathedrals in the pictures their uncle Charlie had shown them from his trip to Europe.

Shelley stood up and stared down at the street. Gray was so predominant in the scene that she could have been staring at a black-and-white photograph. Only the stained glass provided any color, and Shelley deliberately avoided looking at it as her eyes ran over the rest of the scene in the rough-and-tumble neighborhood the youth center occupied the center of.

Three young men in dark jackets added no color to the scene. They stood on the concrete in front of the church without seeming to notice it. Unsavory characters, Shelley felt for some reason. There were many on that street, many in that neighborhood. Many of them would come to see her, as many had before. That was what she was there for.

As she turned, Shelley caught sight of the framed degree on the wall: *Michelle Patricia Vanderberg, Master of Social Work*. She looked back at the young men gathered on the corner and felt her heart constrict. Sometimes she wasn't sure whether working with troubled youth served as a noble catharsis or simply a continuous reminder of a pain she suspected would never go away.

Kenny was in the kitchen when Shelley got home. A lump had formed in her throat, and it took a bit of effort to smile as he greeted her.

Kenny held her gaze a beat longer than usual, and she knew he sensed her discomfort.

"You still want to go, right?" His voice was non-confrontational, and she understood why he asked. She nodded as she draped her coat over a kitchen chair.

"Of course."

Her eyes were downcast as Kenny approached and gently slipped his arms around her. His fingers skimmed over her back, and she leaned into him with a sigh as his hands moved up to her neck, massaging lightly. She was surprised to find that his gentleness, into which she usually melted, seemed to increase her edginess. Her husband's fingers progressed up to her scalp, drifting slowly through her hair.

Shelley caught her breath as she realized she wanted him to pull. Desperately.

She didn't realize she'd murmured the sentiment out loud until he paused and said, "What?" While hair-pulling wasn't something they'd never incorporated into their sex life, Shelley could understand his surprise that she wanted it at that moment.

She did, though. More than almost anything she could think of.

Squeezing her eyes shut, Shelley started to twist away, not knowing how to explain herself. But Kenny held on. She struggled for another second before dropping her head against his shoulder, suddenly at risk of falling if her husband hadn't held her up. His breath was in her ear, and Shelley couldn't keep from squirming a little. She didn't have the energy to try to articulate what she wanted, though, and she stood still, waiting for him to let her go.

Instead Kenny stilled, and she sensed the moment when he understood. All the breath left her body as she felt surprised and not surprised at the same time – of course Kenny knew. He almost always knew.

Silently her husband slid one hand back up to her hair. Gathering a mass in his fist, he gave the slightest pull. Shelley's breath scurried out of reach, staying suspended until he re-grasped a fistful and pulled for real – a sharp, quick tug accompanied by a short exhale into her ear. Shelley's breath shot out as her attention was pulled to her body.

And it was such a relief. Shelley grasped her husband, pushing herself against him as tears rose in her throat. He lowered her to the floor, and she felt as though she were sinking into the carpet as he covered her body with his. Kenny tangled a hand in her hair and pulled again as he kissed her relentlessly, reaching to undo his pants with his other hand. She felt his erection against her thigh as he pulled her skirt up and wrested her panties off.

Despite the firmness of his actions, which Shelley knew he understood she needed right now, she could feel the tenderness in every move he made. She pressed her eyes shut against the tears that pushed out of them, gratitude that her husband knew what to do almost overwhelming her.

Kenny pushed into her, his fingers wrapped in her hair as he kissed her neck, her cheek, her mouth. Her body tingled, coming out of lockdown as tension woke up and dissipated throughout her. The relief brought a sob to the surface, and she wrapped her arms around Kenny's back, squeezing him with arms and legs and cunt as though she could compress the tension out of herself like juice from an orange. Kenny penetrated her harder, his body solid against hers as she willed him to push deeper, deeper, to where he could push all the fear and dread and grief right out of her.

Instead he did what he'd always done – met her where she was, without flinching, and helped her be there too. Shelley held onto him tighter, burying her face in his neck as she let herself be swept by the sensation in her body.

Shelley woke with a start. The powerful dreams she'd been having were repeating themselves, beginning to turn sleep from a welcome reprieve to a fearful endeavor that left her helpless and overwhelmed.

It was the same each time: Swirling colors, a literal rainbow tornado, came ever closer as she ran, sluggishly and powerlessly, away from its unpredictable path. Then Nikki was there, with an expression Shelley couldn't identify or even recognize; when Shelley reached for her, she vanished. Shelley looked back over her shoulder at the frightening spiral of colors. She had never seen a rainbow look threatening before. But there it was, and despite the beauty of its host of colors, she knew it was going to kill her.

Then the piercing blast of shattering glass, acutely attuned to her hearing as though a miniature pane were exploding against her eardrum. The sound in the dream had woken her each time.

Sitting up in bed, Shelley closed her eyes as pings of terror zapped through her like electric pinballs. She'd only had this dream three times. It felt like she had been dreaming it all her life.

Shelley swallowed as she glanced at Kenny, wanting to go back to sleep but afraid to. Her body felt panicked, as if her lungs didn't have the capacity to hold the amount of air she needed to breathe.

When she moved, she found herself curled beside her sleeping husband, clutching at the comforter as she lay with her eyes closed, silent, still, focusing on her breath as it came in and let go, the fundamental act of keeping her body alive.

Right then, breathing was all she could do.

The computer screen glowed in front of her as Shelley stared at it without seeing it. They were leaving for Niagara Falls the next morning, and she was working late, making sure she had everything wrapped up enough with her current cases to take a few days off.

Someone walked by her office, and she looked up, surprised by the movement. Gary similarly backtracked and appeared in her doorway.

"What are you still doing here?" her boss asked.

"Kenny and I leave in the morning, and I'm just making sure everything's in order before I get out of here tonight."

Gary nodded and smiled tiredly, making his gray beard shift as he ran a hand over his balding head.

"What about you?" she asked.

"Oh, I forgot my glasses," he said with a roll of his eyes as he pushed away from the doorframe and continued down the hall toward his office.

Shelley's smile disappeared as her eyes fell to the calendar on her desk. She whirled her chair around and found herself staring at the stained glass windows across the street. The anniversaries were far closer than she would like them to be – which was not at all. Actually, she wished one anniversary simply didn't exist.

For the remainder of their family's inaugural Niagara Falls trip, Nikki had chattered excitedly about how she wanted to open such a butterfly display at home. Given their lack of a greenhouse and the resources to secure exotic butterfly species from around the world, she had had to settle for starting a traditional butterfly collection made up of specimens that were already dead. Upon their return, her sister had enlisted Shelley's help in beginning to collect all the deceased butterflies they could find from the parks and the yards and the sidewalks of their small Ohio town. To this day Shelley had never seen a human action as gentle as Nikki's when she handled the beloved insects, mounting them carefully on the white foam-core board their mother had procured for them from the drugstore.

Shelley jumped as Gary poked his head in again.

"I'm headed out. Have a great time in Niagara Falls, and happy anniversary. See you Monday."

"Thank you." Shelley listened to the muffled scrape of the heavy entrance door as it opened and closed a few seconds later, depositing Gary out into the chill of the Baltimore fall.

The winter after their third year of butterfly collecting, when she had just turned twelve and Nikki was fifteen, something changed. All she'd been told at the time was that Nikki was in the hospital and would be gone for a little while. It wasn't until Shelley overheard a conversation between her parents that she'd walked in and asked what note they were talking about.

Shelley sighed as she turned and stared at the intricacy of the glass-and-iron vision across the street. She didn't doubt her parents had wanted to avoid sharing many details with her, but they had told her what a suicide note was – and that Nikki had written one. Still, despite her parents' careful explanation, she hadn't really understood what was going on. Her parents were obviously distressed, and all Shelley had ended up with was an intense sense of confusion and fear.

Even now Shelley could almost remember the sensation in her stomach when she'd come to understand what might have happened – as well as the feeling of betrayal she'd experienced at that moment more deeply than anything she could ever remember feeling.

Sitting later on Nikki's neatly made bed like a stone, she'd glanced through the open closet door where their butterfly collection was kept. Shelley could still see the striking array of wings, swirls of color and stripes and spots all carefully pinned to the snow-white background.

Shelley swallowed and jerked her chair back around, taking a deep breath to quell the nausea she knew was just outside the edge of her awareness. But there seemed to be little she could do lately to stop the memory reel in her head. Shelley squeezed her eyes shut as she saw herself run to the closet and rake her fingernails down the center of the foamcore, ripping the fragile wings easily as she pulled at the display, sobbing, until the butterflies were no more than a pile of brittle flakes in her lap. Some of the patterns and designs were still discernible as she'd gathered them as best she could in both hands.

Tearing downstairs and out the front door, she'd hurled the contents of her two fists into the smooth snowdrift to the side of the front steps. Despite the force with which she did this, the majority of the butterfly flakes floated peacefully down to land on the snow just inches in front of her. They lay silent and still on the bright white background: shattered angels, showing no resistance.

They never collected butterflies again.

In fact, nothing was ever the same after Nikki came home two weeks later. From that point on, watching her life became like standing by just outside a storm – close enough to feel the stinging spray of the precipitation sometimes, but mostly seeing it like a video on *The Weather Channel*, observing from the outside and worrying about the loved one traveling through the treachery on the screen. Sometimes Shelley would think of the gentle, loving way Nikki had handled the butterflies and wish her sister would act that way toward herself.

Shelley shook herself and stood up. Grabbing her purse, she strode across the office and swung her coat over her shoulders. As her fingers hit the light switch, she paused.

Turning, she looked back across the dark space and through the window. The stained glass was still there, silent and still and the same as it had been for years before she had ever first seen it. Her breathing changed as suddenly she saw the collection of jagged, disparate colored pieces instead of the picture they formed. Unable to tear her eyes away, her gaze traced the edge of each colored glass shard against the pale stone wall, gleaming close to white in the glare of the streetlight.

A far-away siren broke the silence in the dark office. Shelley turned on her heel, pulling the door closed behind her.

Trembling, Shelley sat up in bed. She winced as she felt Kenny stir next to her. They were leaving early in the morning, and she didn't want to wake him. She turned to him just as his eyes opened. He saw her sitting and rose up on his elbow.

"Dream?" He squinted up at her.

She nodded.

"Same one?"

She nodded again.

Kenny sat up beside her and took her hand. "Do you want me to make you some tea?"

Shelley shook her head, not wanting to admit she didn't want him to leave her alone. Her body shook as the memory she had been most avoiding threatened to overtake her consciousness. She squeezed her eyes shut, trying to block out the anniversary so near hers and Kenny's, the dates of which seemed to mesh so close together this year it was as though she was having trouble distinguishing them.

Shelley felt her husband watching her and knew he didn't know what she wanted, how to help her. She fought back panic as the mental energy it took to control her thoughts disintegrated, leaving the elephant in the metaphorical room of her brain to charge mercilessly to the center of it.

The call had come two days after her and Kenny's first anniversary. With a pistol of which no one knew the origin, Nikki had carried out the threat she'd first put in writing all those years ago.

Shelley's eyes were still closed. After a few minutes, she heard her voice emerge as a whisper.

"Fuck me," she whispered.

Kenny hesitated. "What?"

"You heard me."

She had no idea why she suddenly felt like she wanted it so much, but the pull was strong and she didn't question it as she turned to face her husband. She looked at him with desperate eyes, hoping he understood that once again, she needed him to take over.

He studied her for a moment. Then his face cleared, and he reached for her. He lifted her nightshirt over her head and gathered it away from her hair as she sat still. Planting his hands on her shoulders, he eased her back onto the bed. He kissed her cheek, then pulled away to slip his boxers off. Gently but firmly he repositioned her, grasping her waist to slide her up toward the pillows in the center of the bed. After a moment, he pressed on top of her, grasping her hips and sliding into her, fucking her slowly but solidly. Her eyes were closed.

"Harder," she whispered.

He acquiesced, increasing the pace of his thrusting. She lifted her hands and placed them on the pillow on either side of her head, hoping he understood what she wanted.

He did. He grabbed both of them and laced his fingers through them, holding her hands down and fucking her hard, grunting now as his breathing increased. He pulled out and reached to turn her over, and she responded immediately, flipping and rising to her hands and knees. He entered her and grabbed her shoulders, reaching to pull her hair as he fucked her, her breathing fast and heavy as she felt the tension begin to drain out of her.

Kenny reached around and touched her clit. She sucked in her breath, dropping her chin to her chest as Kenny worked her clit with a knowledgeable hand. As he pulled her hair again and she came, not crying out but with her breath ripping through her, the orgasm sweeping through and whisking away the strain and fear in her body. She dropped her cheek to the pillow as it finished, splaying her arms beside her.

Kenny's pace increased. He pounded into her like a determined woodpecker until his breathing told her he was coming. He pulled out, and Shelly lowered herself to the bed, stretching her entire body before rolling over to look up at him.

"Thank you."

Kenny's expression was a mixture of arousal, tenderness, understanding, and concern. She could see it, but she felt far from it somehow as her body trembled a bit from the aftershock of orgasm combined with the undercurrent of fear the physical stimulation had temporarily overridden. Instinctively she reached for him, and he leaned down and kissed her, slowly, lingeringly. She closed her eyes and felt the warmth of it disperse throughout her body.

But even though she didn't feel it right then, she knew the cold was still there.

"I love you." Kenny's whisper slipped into her ear, and she curled harder into him.

"I love you too."

Shelley sat on the plush, snow-white comforter and slid the first of her stockings over her right foot. She focused on not snagging the fabric with her manicured nails as she pulled the nylon up her calf and over her knee, finally adjusting the lace that covered the silicone band where it gripped her thigh. She picked up the other stocking and paused to stare out the window.

It was certainly a view worth pausing for. The honeymoon suite was beyond her expectations. On the trips they'd made as a family when she was a kid, they had never booked a room with a view of the Falls – those were expensive, and they spent enough time out looking at the Falls up close that her parents didn't think they also needed to spend the money to look at them from their window.

At the time, she had agreed and thought little of it. Now she couldn't think of anything more perfect than the view she looked out at from their room on the thirty-fourth floor.

Mist climbed like rising smoke from the stretch of the American Falls to the left. Almost right in front of them were the Horseshoe Falls, the well-deserved Canadian claim to Niagara Falls fame. The water's muted thunder served as a steady background noise in the quiet of the room. Seeing the places she had visited up close numerous times this way afforded a magic she had never known of one of her favorite locations. From her place on the bed, she could see more water than she could land.

The mist that rose from the bottom of the Canadian Falls towered above even their window almost three dozen stories high. The fall sky was overcast, muting the swatches of mustard yellow and burnt orange that swept along the ready-to-turn foliage surrounding the water. It was the first time Shelley had been to Niagara Falls in the fall, her childhood trips having invariably taken place during the summer, when everything surrounding the waters was lush with the vibrant hues of the hottest time of the year.

Her gaze held the constant movement of the water now as it plummeted over the edge, almost paradoxical in the unfaltering motion that made it seem stationary. Shelley pulled on her other stocking, her attention much more on the vision out the window than the garment this time, and her stomach almost turned as she recalled the time she and Nikki had bickered about which one of them got to take pictures with the family camera at the railing she could, surreally, see out their window right now.

Shelley felt her face pale as a sour taste rose in her mouth. She jumped up and turned from the glass, willing her breathing to normalize as she scurried to rummage through the gaping jewelry bag on the vanity counter. She heard the shower stop running as her fingertips brushed tiny bits of metal and beads, feeling for the earrings she had brought just for this evening, their formal anniversary dinner.

She was arranging her blonde hair atop her head when Kenny emerged from the bathroom, freshly shaven with a towel around his waist. Her eyes automatically dropped down his torso as he passed behind her, giving her a wink in the mirror before stepping to pull his suit from the closet. Shelley picked up a bobby pin and pushed it into the hair beneath the fingers of her other hand, willing the unsettledness in her stomach to disappear.

Kenny started to button his crisp white shirt, and as Shelley turned her head to pin another side of her hair, she saw the rainbow. It was the first time she had noticed it, and she lowered her hands and stood up to move closer. The dusky light of the sun had emerged from an unseen break in the clouds, and the transparent colored beam that rose from – or plunged into, depending on how one looked at it – the churning pool at the bottom of the Horseshoe Falls was almost completely vertical.

Kenny looked up from tying his tie and paused in appreciation as well. Feeling an odd juxtaposition of calm and underlying foreboding, Shelley turned from the window and slipped into her red gown, zipping the short zipper in the back and reaching behind her neck to tie the halter ribbons into a bow. Kenny's eyes were on her as she dropped her hands.

"You look breathtaking," he stated.

Shelley looked up into his eyes and smiled. He was fully dressed except for his jacket, his red-and-purple paisley tie as straight as a ruler, black dress shoes shining in the bedside light. He stepped closer. "And I know you're not up for this."

His tone had dropped, and Shelley caught her breath. She opened her mouth to protest, and Kenny closed the space between them and caught her hand. "Shelley."

She didn't know if it was the simplicity of the word, the realness of his touch, the effortlessness of the rainbow out the window, or maybe all three that pulled the pin from the grenade inside her. The tears she suddenly realized had been lying in wait for days burst forth, reflecting the thundering falls outside the window as she nearly collapsed at her husband's feet.

Kenny wasted no time picking her up and settling her onto the bed as she sobbed, her dress crumpling beneath her as she curled herself there, crying without restraint as her husband eased onto the mattress beside her. He let her cry, not interfering but watching her, Shelley knew, with the attention of the only person she'd ever known who knew how to so acutely attune to her, when to help and hold and when to give her space. Her appreciation pushed the tears forth all the harder.

Eventually, without even realizing it, she stopped. Her eyes opened to the glass expanse that covered the wall. Mist rose like steam from a giant tea kettle, silent but for the steady, muted hum of the Falls that created it.

The rainbow had disappeared.

Shelley sat up, feeling somehow lighter and heavy at the same time. "I'm so sorry," she whispered. Her eyes flicked to the digital clock on the nightstand. They would need to leave in ten minutes to be on time for their reservation. Her dress was wrinkled, and she knew without looking that her hair would need a complete redo, not to mention her makeup. Her voice began to crack again as she said, "I didn't mean to ruin our evening."

Then Kenny was beside her, their bodies fitting like the water and rock nestled seamlessly outside the window as he held her against him. It was a few seconds before he spoke.

"You know," he said, "an anniversary isn't 'special.' It isn't some out-of-the-ordinary celebration. Or at least it shouldn't be as far as I'm concerned." He reached for her hand. "We're together. This is what's happening in our lives together right now. That's all an anniversary is." His fingers entered the thickness of her blonde hair. "And that's all I would want it to be."

Shelley exhaled, her eyes downcast.

"Whatever is happening, it's happening with us together, and that's what this is about, Shelley. We don't need dinner or formalwear or anything else to tell us we celebrate our being together. I celebrate it every day."

Shelley fell against him, all resistance expelled as gratitude and grief crashed over her until it was hard to tell which was which. After a few moments, she noticed the hardness beneath Kenny's trousers pressed against her thigh. She shifted to let her hand fall there.

"I'm sorry," Kenny said immediately. She looked up and saw him flush, embarrassed. "I just... love you."

She had often noticed that Kenny seemed particularly turned on in times of profound emotion and connection. She knew it meant he felt especially connected to her right then, and it touched her.

Nonetheless, she didn't seem to have the energy to respond. Smiling softly at him, she nestled back against him and said truthfully, "It's okay."

"I'm sorry again about dinner," she murmured finally, pulling away as she sat up. Automatically she reached to straighten her hair.

"Stop apologizing," Kenny said, reaching for her wrist, "and stop messing with your hair. It looks amazing."

Shelley smiled weakly as she dropped her hands. Her husband went to the phone on the table in the corner, and she breathed a sigh of relief as she heard the low murmur of his voice and knew he was canceling their dinner reservation.

Her gaze landed on the huge white tub as he passed the bathroom on the way back. "Maybe we should try out the whirlpool."

Kenny switched directions and turned on the faucet, launching a miniature version of the thundering phenomenon out the window. As he reached to check the water temperature, Shelley felt a familiar stirring inside her at the sight of his lean figure encased in jet-black dress slacks and white shirt. His tie was still immaculate. The strength of the attraction made her blink as Kenny straightened and came back toward her. Her eyes dropped to the crotch of his trousers to see if his own arousal was still present.

It was.

He saw her looking. When he looked back to meet her eyes, she knew what she was feeling was obvious in hers. And her desire felt different this time; this was not the desperate yearning for distraction and grounding that had been piling up on her so much for the past few weeks. This wasn't that.

She simply wanted him. She wanted her husband.

The awareness made Shelley smile involuntarily, and Kenny looked like he wanted to leap at her. He took a step forward, and she put up her hand.

"Stop," she whispered. She wanted to look at him. She almost said the words out loud, but as she drank in his appearance, the view of the Niagara Falls to her right suddenly taking a distant second, no words came.

"Strip," she finally said. Though it was a command, it came out as a simple word, almost an observation, the softness of a request with no power play on its agenda.

Kenny held her gaze as he lifted his hands to his tie, and she felt herself grow wet as he began to pull it loose, the weight of his eyes like the press of his body against her. Those eyes said more than the visible hardness of his cock how much he wanted her, how precisely he felt the same thing she did as he pulled the tie from around his collar and unbuttoned his top button. She could feel the measured restraint in his slowness, the steadiness that kept him from ripping everything off and pouncing on her. It was the same energy, the same patience, that allowed him the groundedness and perceptivity that so attuned him to, it seemed to her, everything she had ever needed.

He untucked his shirt, and Shelley's breathing grew shallower as each button came undone. She stared unabashedly at his chest, his hands, his crotch, wherever her eyes wanted to take her gaze as he unbuckled his shiny black leather belt.

By the time he was naked, she could feel herself dripping against the red satin she wore. She stood, unsteady, and Kenny took her hand and kissed it before leading her over to the whirlpool. He turned the faucet off, and the silence in the room echoed in her ears as he slid his hands behind her neck and pulled one end of the ribbon there. She heard the slip of the fabric against itself as it untangled, and the front of her dress fell. Kenny maintained his composure with only a visible intake of breath as his eyes dropped to her chest.

Then he grabbed her, smashing her body to his as his fingers wrested her zipper down and he pulled away just enough to let the dress fall to the tile floor. His mouth devoured hers as he grasped her flesh, claiming her waist, her back, her buttocks, her hips. Finally he wrenched away, stepping back to take in the view of her in only her stockings and panties. His eyelids drooped as he stared, and she could almost feel the pulsing of his cock as he gazed at her. It made her blush.

Kenny pushed the button on the wall beside them, and the air jets came bubbling to life. Shelley reached for her panties, but her husband stopped her with the gentle pressure of fingers on her wrist. He stepped into the whirlpool, leaving her standing beside it as he sank into the whirring bubbles. Turning to face her, he pulled her toward the edge of the tub and leaned in to place a kiss on the crotch of her panties.

She drew in a breath as he kept his lips there, the heat of his own exhalation sending tingles throughout her body. Kenny reached up and brushed his palms along her hips, hooking her panties with his thumbs and slowly sliding them down. He let them drop to the floor and pulled her forward until she had to lean and catch herself on the thick silver safety bar along the wall.

Kenny buried his face in her pussy, and Shelley moaned. He pushed his tongue into her, grazing his hands up her inner thighs before replacing his tongue with one finger as he slowly licked her clit. His tongue moved in circles as he worked his finger in and out of her, his other hand squeezing her thigh as she gripped the bar desperately for balance. Impatience overcame her, and she stepped over the edge of the tub into the water. She straddled her husband's face and ground into him. Seconds later, he held her hip to steady her while she came, crying out as her legs shook beneath her.

After the orgasm receded, she fell into the water with a splash, nylon still clinging to her legs. Kenny gasped as she grasped his cock fiercely, pulsing hot water rushing against her forearm as she tugged at him, wanting him, needing him. She pushed at his body, and he read the signal and lifted himself to sit on the edge of the tub.

She dove at his cock, taking it in her mouth with a ravenousness borne of love and gratitude and fierceness, sucking it like it was the very salvation she had so been craving.

"Oh, god, Shel, slow down, you'll make me come."

Kenny barely had the words out before he indeed spurted into her mouth, moaning loudly as she kept sucking, pausing to swallow his liquid heat as it shot into her. Her husband bucked against the wet tile along the edge of the tub, calling out her name as he gripped her shoulders, digging his fingers in with a delicious loss of all composure as Shelley drank the last pulses of his shooting come.

Then she looked up at him, and he slid back into the tub and engulfed her, his breathing heavy as he entwined his legs with hers and she noticed for the first time the blissfulness of the warm currents around them. Her head fell to the crook between his shoulder and his jaw, and his arms came around her, wet fingers caressing tiny circles against the moist skin of her wrist.

The timer on the hot tub stopped, plunging the room into abrupt silence. The bubbles around them dissipated into tiny effervescent streams reaching for the water's surface. Eventually they disappeared.

"Happy anniversary." Kenny's voice cascaded into her ear like quietly falling snow.

Shelley laced her fingers with his and felt the warmth of the bath and the man holding her suffuse every atom of her body. She looked through the smooth water to their naked skin beneath it.

"It is indeed."

Apple Blossoms

"There they are," I said to Brooke, who pulled the straw from her mouth and waved at the group coming in the door. Our friend Scott waved back, and we alerted the staff and made our way from the bar to the rectangular table reserved for our group of eight. "Happy birthday, Bethany," I said to the guest of honor and Scott's wife, giving her a hug as we reached the table. Brooke echoed the sentiment, and there was a general shuffling of chairs as seven people discerned where to sit and placed their belongings accordingly.

"Courtney called and said she's on her way," Scott said to the table at large as Bethany seated herself at one end of it. "And Brooke and Ashley, I'd like you to meet Brad, one of Bethany's and my friends from our co-ed softball league. Brad, this is Brooke and Ashley." There was a hint of severity in the look Scott shot his friend as Brooke and I stepped forward to shake his hand.

Brad appraised us with barely disguised enthusiasm. "Nice to meet you," he said, giving us both a once-over as he sat down across from the chair Brooke dropped into. As soon as I was seated, he said, "So, how long have you two been together?"

"About five years."

"Five years. Huh." Brad sat back in his chair. Scott had obviously told him about us, though I didn't know how much he'd said. I found out when Brad continued.

"So do you go both ways then, or just girls?" He addressed the question to both of us, and immediately I knew how to account for the look Scott had given him during the introductions.

"Is that a common icebreaker question of yours?" Brooke asked, her smile sedate.

"I just find you both hot," Brad responded as though that somehow constituted an answer. "I'd do both of you in a heartbeat, so I was just wondering what the chances were of my getting to join you in a threesome tonight." He winked, and I had little doubt the charm that emanated from his blue eyes had historically served him well in tempering a characteristic audacity.

"How interesting that you seem to assume that our relationship is non-monogamous, and also that there's nothing inappropriate about intimating to both of us, in each other's presence, that you want to fuck her respective partner. Do you usually tell people you want to fuck them when their partner is sitting right there?" Brooke's tone was mild, and I knew she wasn't speaking antagonistically but rather capitalizing on an opportunity to enlighten.

Brad looked confused, then considered for a moment. He shrugged. "I guess you're right. Sorry."

I smiled, nudging Brooke's foot affectionately under the table. Brad's comment wasn't anything we hadn't heard the likes of before, but that didn't inoculate me from finding it annoying. One of the many things Brooke and I had in common was a keen interest in the demolition of sexual and gender stereotypes, superficial assumptions about lesbian relationships being high on the list.

It happened that Brooke and I did not define our partnership as strictly monogamous, though our respective play beyond the relationship had tapered considerably in the last few years. While both our multi-partnered and kinky proclivities had flared with gusto during the first couple years we were together, for the past few such outside interaction had maintained a contented trickle. Our kinky play as well was now practiced almost solely between the two of us, and as often as not, our sex was vanilla.

But that was all by conscious and considered choice, and the inclination, desire, and experience were still there for both of us if the opportunity arose. When Brooke caught my eye, there was a gleam in hers that I recognized. I held back a smile. The proposal I saw in them was something we hadn't done in a while, probably a couple years if I remembered correctly. But that gleam told me she felt the opportunity had arisen.

With my look back, I answered.

Brooke smiled and turned back to Brad. "As it happens, the two of us have occasionally engaged in such a configuration. But you may not feel comfortable with the kind of things Ashley and I have been known to incorporate into our sex life."

"Like what?" He was immediately interested again.

"Some things some people might consider a little rough. Bondage. Strap-ons."

"Well, I guess I'm not surprised you use strap-ons," he said with a lopsided grin, and I resisted the urge to roll my eyes. *Brad, Brad, Brad*, I thought. *You could really use a little bit of a wake-up call – as well as perhaps a crash course in sensitivity.*

Brooke was wearing a barely-hidden smirk that anyone who knew her would recognize. Brad, of course, didn't know her, so his obliviousness continued as she spoke again. I sat with my glass in my hand, content, as was not uncommon, to let her do most of the talking. Despite the kinky and multi-partnered activities in my past, both with Brooke and before I met her, in both social and sexual settings I tended to be somewhat shy. Brooke and I switched, and I was fully capable of dominating her on occasion, but around groups and whenever more than the two of us had been involved, I was usually content to let Brooke lead the way.

"So we'd want anyone who joined us to be interested in those things too," Brooke continued.

"Great!" Brad practically drooled into his beer, and I almost laughed out loud.

"You're comfortable with that kind of thing?"

"Yeah, whatever you want!"

Brooke's smile held just enough of an edge to let anyone listening know she was serious. "Don't you think you might want to be careful giving someone you don't even know that kind of carte blanche in a sexual setting?"

For the first time, Brad blushed, and I wondered what was really going on inside his head. I suspected what

Brooke had in mind, and I suspected as well that Brad might not be as thrilled as he anticipated were he to be aware of it.

With that blush, for some reason, I wondered if I was wrong.

Scott turned our way then from the conversation he'd been having with the other half of the table. "And what's going on down here?" he asked with a swig of his drink, his gaze flitting from Brad to me to Brooke. Instantly he registered Brooke's expression, and his eyes went back to Brad. I saw the wariness in them as he let the question dangle, this visual assessment seeming to have increased his interest in the answer.

"Just getting to know each other," I said with a wink.

"I see. Can I get anyone another drink?" Scott stood up and glanced down at us as Brad and Brooke both relayed a request. I thanked him with a shake of my head, and he turned and headed for the bar.

Brooke engaged in answering a question from our friend Peggi, who was sitting on the other side of her, and Brad turned to respond to a comment from Bethany. Our interrupted conversation slid away like a silk scarf slipping from a table, and I sat back and sipped my drink. Scott returned and handed one glass to Brad and set another on the table before sliding a chair down to sit by me.

"How's it going?" he asked.

"Fine." I grinned at him.

"Is Brad acting like an ass?" The question made me laugh out loud, and Scott continued. "I mentioned you guys to him ahead of time specifically to ask him to not act like an idiot, as I've certainly seen him do. Seriously, has he said anything truly offensive? He's a good guy – just needs a little education about some things. But I'll certainly get him out of here if it's a problem."

I waved my hand dismissively. "No, it's no big deal. Brooke handled it."

Scott chuckled. "I don't doubt it," he said as he stood up. "All right, I just wanted to say hi." I waved as he squeezed between the chairs back to his seat at the other end of the table.

When the bill had been paid and the party started to break up, Brooke kissed my cheek as we stood to say our goodbyes. Catching Brad staring, she looked directly at him and said, "Would you like to come with us, Brad?"

"Hell yeah." Brad almost dropped his glass in his rush to set it down. He stood up, a cocksure demeanor indicating that perhaps he really had assumed the invitation would be forthcoming all along. I shook my head to myself.

"You're ready to join in however we ask? Because I can assure you, Brad, you won't just be watching." Brooke's smile was calm, her gaze on Brad steady.

"Of course I want to join in." He looked as if she'd asked if he'd be willing to win the lottery, and I spoke up.

"Even if what we do seems a little... unorthodox?"

He grinned at me, his blue eyes sparkling as he said, "You bet, sweetheart. I'd love the chance to get into whatever you two have going on."

I saw Brooke's smile widen. She gave him a nod, and I turned and followed as she led the way to the door.

Brad may not have bargained for the position he found himself in two hours later in our spare bedroom, but I knew Brooke felt the same way I did: The second he wasn't enjoying it, it wouldn't be happening.

Once away from the scene at the restaurant, Brad appeared a little nervous, as well as unsure. Despite his enthusiasm, I didn't doubt that he had no idea what to do after he followed us into the entry way of our home. Of course, even if he had, what I knew Brooke had in mind would likely have looked considerably different from what he expected.

After going over safe words and the talk about everything being consensual, Brad began to resume the boldness we had observed at the table.

"Great," he said as he sat back against the living room couch with a grin. "So you two are just going to go at it then, and I'll join in as soon as I can't stand it anymore and finish the job?" He gave me a wink, and I smiled back at him.

Before Brooke could speak, I did it for her: "I don't think that was quite the way we were seeing it."

He raised his eyebrows, the smile still in place, and said, "Well, let me in on the secret then, ladies. How do you picture this going down?"

Brooke smiled as she stood up. "I'm glad you asked, Brad. Follow me, please."

She led the way into the spare bedroom, flicking on the low lamp on the bedside table. In the middle of the room was a spanking bench covered in burgundy leather padding. She pulled a coil of silver rope from the chest at the foot of the bed.

In the low light, Brad did indeed looked a bit taken aback. "Wow. So which one of you gets tied up?" he asked, looking at the two of us.

Brooke chuckled softly. "Neither."

Confusion flickered over Brad's face for an instant before understanding replaced it, and for the first time, he looked unabashedly surprised. There was silence in the room for several seconds.

"What happens then?" Brad's voice was thick.

"We'll show you," Brooke said, lifting a pair of harnesses from the chest before handing me my realistic-style dildo from it. Brad watched as she retrieved her own jet-black silicone toy and closed the chest. "I'll give you a hint though: These strap-ons may not be put to quite the use you were envisioning during our earlier conversation."

Brad's eyes widened, and I knew this was the moment of truth: the make or break time when he agreed or not, when he had the absolute option to stop this train before it started and walk right back out the door. The heat in the room seemed to elevate as we watched him. I had truly no idea what he would choose.

When he moved forward, his eyes on the bench, I remembered suddenly his blush at the restaurant. The memory checked the surprise I felt as he ran his fingers over the burgundy padding and slowly began to take off his shoes.

Brooke rested a hand now on the small of Brad's back as she positioned the black dildo between his buttocks. She rubbed it back and forth against his opening, the liberally applied lube further smearing along his skin.

It was I that was watching, though not for long. I stood in front of Brad, who was draped over and bound to the bench in the center of the room. I was almost naked, wearing only my black demi bra and a harness to which the silicone dildo Brooke had handed me was secured.

Brooke ran her fingers over Brad's hips, waiting, among other things, for his muscles to relax. I watched as she spoke to him in soft tones, holding the dildo firm against his opening. Her chest was flushed, her skin dewy beneath the vinyl harness I hadn't seen her wear for a while.

She looked up and met my eyes. I caught my breath as desire sizzled through me.

Knowing she was waiting for me, I moved forward, as though to get closer to her, though it was Brad's mouth I was approaching. I maintained eye contact with my girlfriend until I felt the heat from Brad's breath against my thighs. Still looking at her, I set my hand on his head. His blond hair was smooth beneath my fingers.

With a little grin, Brooke broke eye contact and looked down at the back of Brad's head. I dropped my eyes to where he looked up at me. His gaze was wary, but beneath the humility I saw a hunger. It was that hunger – the part beneath the façade, beneath what he displayed regularly and perhaps even consciously knew was there – that I looked back at as I called it forth silently, waiting as it overtook the last bit of hesitation in his eyes. Whether this was something he would have thought he'd wanted, whether he would want it in an hour, or next week, or ever again under any circumstances besides those that had coalesced into this moment, I didn't know. I'd guess he didn't either.

But the look in his eyes as he looked up at me said he wanted it now. And that was all I needed.

I looked up at Brooke and nodded. She set a hand on Brad's body and eased the black dildo into him. A sound came from his throat, and she pushed in further at the same measured pace before withdrawing just as slowly. I watched as she continued to penetrate him, slowly, waiting for him to get used to the sensation, for them both to grow comfortable with the rhythm. Heat simmered inside me as I watched the smooth motion of Brooke's strong hips.

I tightened my grip on Brad's soft hair as I looked back down at him. With my other hand, I grasped the silicone cock strapped to my body and touched it to his lips. They opened easily, and I groaned as though there really were nerve endings in the toy connected to me as I slid it into his mouth. My pussy tingled, arousal gathering in my clit as I pulled my hips back and slid them forward again slowly. Like Brooke, I was finding the rhythm, and while fucking his mouth certainly didn't require the same delicacy as fucking his ass, I didn't doubt he wasn't used to this and didn't want to overwhelm him.

Brooke sped up her pace, observing Brad's muscles closely. I knew she was watching for any tension, anything that would indicate that he wasn't enjoying himself or that would cause discomfort as he took what she was giving him.

"Are you enjoying yourself, Brad?" she asked as she smacked his ass. "Are we making all your fantasies come true?" Her face had broken a sweat, her stylishly cropped blonde hair damp around her ears. The vision of her confident handling of Brad as well as her own obvious arousal had my pussy nearly dripping.

"I think he's liking it more than he may admit," she said to me, leaning down to reach beneath his body just behind the bench. She sent me a wink that pooled the heat between my legs further, and I jammed the dido into Brad's mouth, careful not to hurt him, as I found a rhythm that made the base of the silicone press against my clit just so.

I moaned as I moved my body closer and closer to orgasm. In seconds I screeched and bucked wildly as I came, backing away from Brad and sliding my fingers beneath the harness to replace the rhythm my bucking hips had created. Circling my clit frantically, I dropped to my knees as the climax tore through me, toppling my ability to stand.

I opened my eyes and looked across at Brooke, who had slowed down her own action to take in the view of my orgasm. The heat from her gaze seared into me, and I fell forward, panting, as my hand dropped slowly from my body.

I moved my eyes to Brad, whose gaze shot pure lust back at me as he took in my post-orgasmic state like a lion feasting on flesh. Brooke looked down at him as well, clasping his hips as she steadied herself and prepared to pull out.

"Have you had about enough, darling?" she asked him. She backed up, removing the toy from his ass, and unfastened her harness. Her face was glowing with exertion and arousal, her blonde hair clamped to her forehead in little wet clusters. She was out of breath, her slim figure heaving as she removed the harness and stood still, allowing her body to regain its equilibrium.

She looked gorgeous.

I watched her from my knees as she stepped forward and began to undo the rope around one of Brad's ankles. Momentarily I rose to help, allowing my breasts to dangle inches from his face as I undid one of the knots binding his wrists. I looked down to find his eyes glued to my tits, his breath audible as I untied the other wrist and Brooke invited him to stand up.

He stood in front of us, an unquestionable humility reflected in his eyes, his chest moving perceptibly as he finished catching his breath. I dropped my eyes to his granite-hard cock. A drop of pre-come glistened on the end of it, and I couldn't help smiling. Cocks didn't do a lot for me in and of themselves, but it was fun to be involved with someone's so obvious and acute arousal. I looked at Brooke, no idea what was on the agenda now.

"It looks to me like you want to get off. I guess that makes sense – that's what this little escapade was all about for you, wasn't it?" Brooke smiled cheerfully at Brad, who blushed a little as he swallowed. "Do you want to come?" Brooke asked when he remained silent.

Brad nodded, hurriedly, as though the answer was obvious but he had been afraid to state it. Which, I guessed, was exactly the case.

Brooke indicated his cock, a slow grin encompassing her features. "Go ahead."

He looked at her hesitantly. I looked at her too. Brooke stood back, arms crossed, and I finally understood that she was prompting him to jack himself off while we watched.

I bit my lip, suddenly eager for something I had never found the slightest bit appealing. I wondered if it would please Brooke, and I realized that possibility was part of what turned me on.

Brad seemed to be waiting for further direction – either that, or he felt reluctant to start with our watching him. Ignoring him, I sidled over to Brooke and pressed against her naked body. I whispered into her ear, and she gave me a surprised smile. I blushed, knowing I seemed out of character – not just in the action I suggested but also in initiating, in wanting to do something different and impulsive like I watched her enthuse over all the time.

"Well that's great, Ashley," Brooke said out loud. "Why don't you go right ahead and do that." She turned to Brad. "Ashley wants to kneel in front of you and have you come all over her tits." She ran a hand over my breast, squeezing lightly, and I ducked my head shyly.

I leaned forward and kissed her, briefly, and as I started to pull away she grabbed me and pulled me back toward her with a kiss that started fast and hard, her lips and tongue and mouth surging against mine, and transformed gradually and organically into the softness I saw in her sometimes, when her blonde hair became like a gentle light illuminating a face not devoid of her usual boisterousness but incorporating into it a sincerity, a gentle and exquisite caring. It wasn't something foreign to her – even when it didn't appear to be there, I knew it was, as an integral part of her that simply tended to stay quieter than the impulsiveness and enthusiasm – but whenever I experienced it so openly, so close to the surface like this, it was like being wrapped in emotional velvet, a softness exuding from her to me to everything around us, holding all of it in a lightness that, for a moment, overtakes the world.

When she had first grabbed me I'd wondered if the kiss was partly for Brad's benefit, and whether it had been or not, by the end I knew it was for no one's – not even ours. It wasn't a "benefit" kind of kiss. It was just something that happened, like the opening of an apple blossom.

I opened my eyes slowly after we broke apart. With a soft smile Brooke released my hands, which she'd been holding, and turned slowly back toward Brad. I followed suit, and he met my eyes as I looked at him, standing motionless with his hand positioned around his cock. His eyes shot fiery lust, and it occurred to me that he had just gotten a little bit of what he had originally wanted. I wondered if it had the same effect following his recent experience.

Holding his gaze, I stepped forward until I was almost touching him. He looked down at me, his jaw clenching and unclenching as I felt the heat from his body sweep over and blend with my own. I reached back and unhooked my bra, sliding my hands around my sides as I nudged the garment from my breasts and let it drop to the floor. His eyes fell to my tits, and he swallowed as he looked back up at me. For a moment, neither of us moved.

I dropped to my knees. Brad groaned, his head falling back as he gripped his cock tight in a fist, barely jerking it twice before his hot come shot straight onto my exposed tits, his volume increasing as he looked back down to see my fingertips sliding delicately over the slickness on my skin, watching the glistening surface with fascination as his face contorted and his hand tugged desperately at his cock. Automatically he reached to put a hand on my shoulder for balance but caught himself before he did. Understanding his hesitation, I smiled and reached for his hand, bracing my palm against his to help hold him up as his last drops of come landed on my body.

Unexpectedly I felt Brooke grasp my tits from behind, and I gasped. I turned my head to see her kneeling behind me, her lips hot against the back of my neck as her hands smeared through the come covering my chest to squeeze my nipples. A tiny whimper escaped me, and I let go of Brad's hand as my girlfriend grasped my body and devoured my neck with an urgency I felt suddenly on fire to experience once the two of us were alone.

Gradually Brooke released me, landing one more kiss at the top of my spine before she stood and reached to help me up. Brad stood panting in front of us, his expression a stupor of release and incredulity.

"Well, Brad, it's been a pleasure," Brooke purred, standing close to him as she looked up into his eyes. "I hope you enjoyed yourself."

Brad looked like he didn't know how to respond, or perhaps had not yet recovered his faculty of speech, and I stepped forward to rest a hand on Brooke's hip.

"Thanks for joining us," I said. "It had been a while since we'd done that."

"Really?" Brad let slip a moment of vulnerability, and he blushed. "I mean, have you... you've done that before?"

"Not quite like that." Brooke smiled. "You were a first."

Brad smiled too, and I sensed the moment when all facades among us dropped. "It was a first for me too," he said quietly. He turned to gather his clothes, and Brooke and I stood still as we watched him begin to dress.

Then she turned to me silently, pressing her body to mine with a kiss that instantly reignited the heat that rushed to my pussy. I slid my hands up her body and cupped her breasts, sensing her breath catch as I squeezed them, gently at first, then more firmly.

We were breathless as we broke apart. I turned to Brad, who was facing us as he fastened his belt.

"Thank you both," he said. His nod seemed a bit wistful, and I knew he was aware that Brooke and I were going to continue without him after he was gone – and that he understood why he wasn't invited. I knew also that it was an understanding that wouldn't have occurred to him a few hours before, and it endeared him to me.

I stepped forward to give him a hug. "It was very nice to meet you, Brad."

He smiled down at me, and I felt understanding in Brooke's hand as she took mine as we followed him to the door.

"Perhaps you could come back and play with us again sometime," she said as we reached it, giving my hand a squeeze.

I squeezed back as Brad turned around. "I'd love to," he said, his smile the most sincere I'd seen from him. Brooke and I stepped forward to give him a kiss on either cheek, and he waved and slipped out the door.

"Funny how much more likeable he was after he was humbled," Brooke said.

"Most of us are," I answered, already pulling my girlfriend back toward the bedroom. "Come, my love. We've got a job to finish."

Rain Check

I felt Luke's hand between my legs almost immediately as I slid into the passenger seat. I gasped and bit my lip, turning to him with a surprised smile. He didn't look at me, just sat with a contented look on his face as he guided his SUV out of the parking lot. Our lunch date at the state park near our workplaces hadn't been quite as successful as we both would have liked, a fellow park patron walking his dog having happened by just as I was bent over a picnic table begging Luke to fuck me. As we'd walked back to the vehicle, I'd slipped the condom I'd transferred to my jacket pocket back into my purse, reluctantly accepting that we'd have to take a rain check.

Luke, however, apparently wanted to make the most of the little time we had left together before we had to go back to our respective offices. I had worn no panties for our little tryst, so it was easy for him to delicately caress my clit now as he watched the traffic in front of him. It wasn't near rush hour yet, but there were plenty of other cars reflecting the afternoon sun around us as we stopped for a red light.

I put my sunglasses on. I was starting to squirm in the seat now, in part to keep my wetness from getting on the leather underneath me. I turned to look at Luke again. He glanced my way and smiled casually, appearing not at all out of the ordinary, I was sure, to the numerous drivers and passengers surrounding us who might glance out their window and have no idea that his fingers were working me into near oblivion beside him. I wasn't quite close to coming, but his slow massaging felt so good I almost felt like I was floating. I would have been perfectly satisfied if he had said we were taking a road trip to Alaska, as long as he was planning to keep that hand where it was for the duration.

The light turned, and he accelerated with everyone else. I pressed my head back against the headrest, letting out a tiny moan as I gave up trying to keep the seat clean and relaxed into the leather, knowing a mess was already being made though I hadn't even come.

Finally he spoke. "So... I've been told, Renee my dear," he began, glancing over his shoulder as he merged into the left turn lane, "that I'm even more effective with my tongue than my fingers. So if you're enjoying this..." He trailed off as he removed his hand momentarily to make the turn, his eyes on the road ahead.

I caught my breath at the suggestion. Luke repositioned his hand and accelerated to cruising speed. I swallowed and looked away shyly. I didn't consider it in my nature to be shy, especially sexually, but on that subject it was undeniable that there had always been a mysterious hesitation in me. We had been dating for four months, and this was the first time the subject had come up so directly. I'd had the impression a number of times that he had wanted to go down on me, but I had always managed to divert his attention and avoid the subject.

It occurred to me that perhaps the time had come for me to suck it up and deal with it directly. Squirming a little for reasons other than the pleasure between my legs, I said uncomfortably, "Well..." I didn't get much further for a few moments.

He looked my way, eyebrows raised over the lenses of his sunglasses, waiting for me to continue.

I fidgeted with my fingers. "I don't usually let people do that," I finally finished.

He nodded slowly, eyes on the road, and said, "Any particular reason?"

I fidgeted more. There wasn't really "any particular reason," except for a vague self-consciousness that I didn't really know the origin of, much less how to explain in this context. In conversation, I had no trouble spouting off about gender socialization and how women weren't socialized to embrace their sexuality, and specifically how oral sex on women being much less talked about and more socially taboo than oral sex on men was an example of that, etc., etc. – all of which I believed but which didn't seem to fit the context when I found myself in the midst of this uncomfortable conversation. Furthermore, I didn't like to think of myself being in the category of women who had any trouble embracing their sexuality. It was hard to conclude, however, that the self-consciousness I felt about the topic at hand was not an indication that socialization had gotten the better of me somewhere along the line. It was an idea I entertained with no amount of pride whatsoever.

I returned to the conversation. "Um... I just... I don't know." The more I wasn't coming up with anything comprehensive, the more self-conscious I was getting. As well as frustrated – we'd been together for four months, for crying out loud. Why would I still feel uncomfortable about this?

"I guess I don't understand why you'd want to," I blurted out. I felt like a traitor to my sex as I said it, but having no sexual attraction to women myself, I had never understood how the act could be appealing.

He chuckled. "Don't you like to do it to me?" he asked.

"Yes," I answered immediately. And I did. I loved to give blow jobs, craved it, salivated for the feel of his cock in my mouth and hot come shooting all over my face.

"Then what wouldn't you understand?" Luke altered the motion of his finger on my clit just enough to make me catch my breath before I could answer.

"I just... I'd have to feel like you really wanted to do it," I said finally. "I wouldn't want you to do it just because you think I'd want you to. I'd want you to really *want* to do it." I took a deep breath. I wasn't sure that even made sense to me, much less that it would make sense to anyone else listening. We'd stopped at a red light again, and Luke took the opportunity to look at me, lowering his head to meet my gaze over his sunglasses.

"Okay, well I'll tell you this right now. I won't keep harping on it in the future, but I want this to be clear to you: I always want to." The words sent a jolt through me, and I almost came right then. He continued without breaking his gaze. "That's not ever a question. It's something I love to do, and I've been thinking about doing it to you since the first time I saw you. It's up to you – but don't ever let my desire be in question."

The cars in front of us started to move, and after holding my gaze for another beat, Luke turned back to the road. I shivered a little at the intensity of his gaze as well as at his words, and suddenly I found myself turned on by the idea like I had never been before. We were quiet for the five remaining minutes of the drive back to his office, his finger gently stroking my clit until he pulled his hand away to shift into park.

When I kissed him goodbye, he said, "I was thinking. Since our park escapade was so abruptly interrupted today, I'd like to take you back this evening when we might be able to... finish what we started." He winked at me, and I grinned back. "We'll just try to find a spot a little less populated this time. I'll be wrapping up about 6:00 – can you meet me back here after you get off work?"

"Sure." I got out and wiggled my hips to adjust my skirt, feeling the slickness between my legs as I turned and walked to my car. Looking once over my shoulder to catch Luke watching my ass, I laughed and blew him a kiss before dropping into the driver's seat.

Returning to the same parking lot a few hours later, I again felt the wetness between my legs just thinking about our earlier encounter. I watched Luke emerge from the building and met him at his vehicle. He kissed me and threw his briefcase into his backseat, and I once again positioned myself in the passenger seat, smiling a little as I thought of our ride back earlier in the afternoon. We inched through rush hour traffic until he turned off the main highway to the road that led to the state park.

He parked in a different lot, smaller and further back in the woods, and we got out under the shade of a cluster of huge oak trees, the sun almost completely blocked by the branches above. I grabbed a blanket from the back and followed him along a trail beneath densely packed trees. Eventually there was a clearing where the sun blazed uninterrupted to the ground a bit off the path. A huge rock sat on the far side of the grassy hill, and we crossed over to it and spread the blanket at its base.

No pretense of eating this time, we fell to the ground, kissing hard. Luke rolled on top of me, pinning me down as his lips moved to my throat, working their way up my neck until they found my ear.

"I want to lick your pussy," he whispered, and I jumped ever so slightly. Partly, I couldn't deny, because of the eroticism of the comment. My pussy, without any input from me, got wetter at the words. In the next instant, however, I felt the familiar self-consciousness sweep in and overcome.

Luke pulled my chin firmly with one finger to look at him when I ducked my head. "You don't have to let me if you don't want to. If you don't want it, that's fine. But please don't say no because you think *I* don't want to." He traced his finger lightly from my chin down to between my breasts, raising goosebumps all over my body. "Because I'm begging you," he continued softly, flicking his tongue out to nip my slightly open lips. He moved his mouth back to my ear and whispered into it, "I want to lick you to climax."

My breath caught. "I don't think you'd be able to do that," I managed to get out. "No one ever has..." Internally, I knew that might be because I had allowed very few people to try – and when I had, I had been so uncomfortable that I had known from the start that there was almost no way I was going to come.

"Then just let me lick it," he breathed into my ear, his hand snaking between my legs to my naked pussy again. I was wet from the conversation, and my breathing deepened as Luke started circling my clit again with his finger. "I want to taste you." Gently he pushed me back on the blanket and started to move.

"No," I said suddenly, sitting partially up. He looked at me.

"Why," he asked evenly, his finger returning to my clit. "Is it because of what you want or because you're worried about what I'm thinking?"

We both knew the answer, and Luke didn't wait for me to give it before moving to position himself between my legs. I was still propped up on my elbows, looking anxiously at him as he stared at my pussy for several seconds. I bit my lip.

Finally he looked up at me and smiled softly. "Your pussy is so gorgeous," he said. I looked at him, wondering if I could dare to believe him – dare to allow myself to relax and trust that he loved this, that he wanted to do it. That there was nothing there to be afraid of. In that split second as I looked in his eyes, sure that he knew what I was thinking, I felt myself lowering back to the ground, my legs opening almost imperceptibly further, nonverbally giving him permission. Giving myself permission.

Luke moaned against me as he replaced his finger with his tongue. I stiffened for just a second, some vague nervousness resurfacing in me, but he put his hands gently on the insides of my thighs, and I felt the reassurance in them. Relaxing again, I closed my eyes and let myself experience, let myself feel what was happening just like I did when he fingered me or fucked me or all the other things I loved when he did to me.

Without even realizing it I stopped worrying – his enthusiasm was evident. My attention then went to the sensation in my clit, the way it felt as his warm tongue feathered across it, my hands in his hair and both of his on my thighs. I arched my back as the floaty sensation returned and flowed through me, a comfort I'd never felt before when receiving oral sex resting in me.

As I started writhing, Luke pulled back an inch or two and whispered, his hot breath against my pussy, "I want you to come." As with our earlier conversation, arousal shot through me at the words, but at the same time my nervousness returned.

"Huh-uh," I whimpered, trying to raise myself up again.

"Mm-hmm," the word vibrated against my pussy as he sucked my clit lightly. The sensation made me weak, but I couldn't stand the thought of coming while he was down there. I had been known to squirt, and the thought of making a mess all over him mortified me.

"No, Luke, stop," I pleaded, my voice weak but the intention sincere. Luke pulled away enough to look up at me.

"Renee. Please. I don't want to stop. I want to make you come," his tone was pleading as well, but I couldn't handle the idea yet. I shook my head.

"No, honey. I'm sorry."

After looking at me for another few seconds, Luke sighed and hoisted himself back up to lie beside me.

I felt myself blushing. Luke ran a finger along my cheek and said, "Thank you."

"For what?"

"Letting me do that," he answered.

I looked dubious. He raised his eyebrows.

"Did you really like it?" I asked almost inaudibly.

He let out a short laugh. "Was it not obvious that I loved it?" When I didn't answer, he said my name, and I looked at him.

"I loved it," he said, looking in my eyes.

I took a deep breath. It was hard, actually, not to believe him.

"Now let me make you come," he said suddenly in my ear, moving back down between my legs before I even realized what was happening.

"Luke – no! Luke," I gasped as he pushed his face into my pussy again. "Luke – honey, stop it!" I heard the urgency in my voice. There was a serious possibility that I would actually come soon, I knew. I didn't think it would happen without an active psychological release on my part, but I still didn't want to take the chance. I tried to pull away but Luke anchored his arms around my thighs and held me in place as he ran his tongue frenetically over my clit. As I felt myself on the brink and tried to resist, he looked up and said, "Come for me, Renee. Now. I want your come all over my face."

And I was too far gone for the worry to supersede the erotic jolt of his words this time. He returned to my clit, and in another spilt-second decision I let the wave come, feeling the orgasm burst throughout my body as I screamed and bucked, his tongue pulsing in place and his arms tight around my thighs. I didn't squirt, to my relief, but I was immediately overcome by confusion, self-consciousness, ecstasy, and something I didn't even recognize as the orgasm ended, and as Luke once again rose to lie beside me, I found myself in tears.

He was quiet as he watched them fall. He wrapped his arms around me, and I cried freely as I had come freely, letting what was there come out as it needed to.

Soon I was still. Luke asked me if I was okay, and I smiled because I knew I was. I didn't know how to explain to him yet that the mix of intensity, intimacy, and pleasure had simply overwhelmed me. And somewhere in there too was relief, though I didn't know how to explain that yet either – even to myself. I touched his face lightly and then pushed my head into his shoulder, pressing against him as he squeezed me and stroked my back. I felt him kiss the top of my head, then pull away slightly.

"Oh – we've got company," he said, sitting up and pulling my skirt down quickly. I turned and saw a young couple with an energetic lab on a leash walking the path 100 yards away. "What is with the dog-walkers today?" he continued as I laughed. "I guess that's what we get for continuing to do this in parks. Think they saw us?" he asked, turning back to me.

I looked in his hazel eyes, the answer in me long before it made its way to my voice.

"I hope so."

No Such Thing

"What moves you?"

Casey frowned a little, moving her focus inside, trying to answer this question from her breathworker. Laurie looked at her, not really expectantly, but with a soft emphasis, one that compelled her to take the question seriously. What moved her? She had little doubt that Laurie was guiding her, and most likely somewhere she needed to go, but Casey found she didn't know what the question meant.

Laurie continued. "I know you want to help Jason. The truth is, the most effective thing we can do to help others be healthy and whole is to be healthy and whole ourselves. When we are aligned with the life force that is always in us, healing and growth occur naturally. From that an intrinsic energetic momentum is created that invites those things in others as well."

Casey tried to take in Laurie's words. She had started breathwork several weeks ago out of a kind of desperation, a yearning for something to help her deal with the pain of her and Jason's separation, with Jason's affliction and the searing feeling that she had no way to help him. An acquaintance at her yoga class had introduced her to breathwork, explaining it as a healing modality that focused on the breath as the connection between the individual (form) and the universe (spirit) and as such the basis for profound physical, emotional, mental, and spiritual healing and transcendence.

"I'd like you to ponder that question," Laurie said as she began arranging the mat on the floor for the breathing portion of the session. "What really moves you, deep inside, beyond what you perceive as obligation, what you 'should' do or are 'supposed' to do. Be still and allow yourself to look beyond those internal commands and see what is really there. That's where your power is. That is where you will feel your alignment with the universe and its complete unconditional support of you."

Casey felt an inexplicable unease. "What if it's something that's not supposed to move me?"

Laurie smiled. "If it's authentic – if you receive it when you are still, not from your mind's ingrained patterns and habits but rather from *now*, a spontaneous arising from the stillness inside you – then there is no such thing."

As she pulled into the garage, Casey glanced at the empty place where Jason's Jeep used to be. For a moment she recalled an evening not long ago when they had arrived home at the same time. Jason had jumped out and met her as she got out of her car. After a quick kiss, he had promptly bent her over the hood of his jeep, leaving her gasping with surprise and laughter as he hiked up her skirt and entered her before the garage door had even fully closed.

Her body tingled as she pictured the scene, his breath hot on her neck, her squeals of surprise turning to eager moans as he started pounding into her from behind. Grasping her hair, he had pulled her head back and run his fingers up her neck ever so lightly before sliding them to her lips, where her tongue nipped over his skin as the garage light faded into darkness. The heated sound of their breathing had seemed to intensify in the pitch blackness as Jason thrust deeper inside her, wrapping his arms solidly around her body from behind.

Casey jumped now as the phone rang inside. She shook herself and stepped through the door to answer it.

"Jason is having trouble," Jessie, her sister-in-law, said softly after greeting her. Casey took a deep breath, and Jessie continued after a pause. "He was definitely intoxicated when I got there last night."

Casey closed her eyes as a painful jolt lurched through her. He was trying so hard, she knew. She knew how much Jason wanted to be sober, wanted his life to be his own again.

Their separation was three months old. She had tried everything in her power to help him for the last two years, as alcohol had gradually taken her place as the thing he prioritized over all else in his life. She felt that if he would just open up to her, let her be there for him, she would be. But he didn't give her a chance. He would face the drug's savage takeover of his being before he would face the reality of needing support. Finally she knew couldn't stand by helplessly anymore while he shut her out and perpetrated his own unhealth through the poison of not only alcohol but also the harsh repression she knew it took for him to seem so unfeeling all the time. She knew that repression hurt him. She wondered if he did.

As Jessie continued talking, Casey squeezed her eyes shut and reminded herself that she couldn't fix him. Reopening them, she reached for the tea kettle and abruptly noticed she wasn't breathing. Laurie had mentioned something like that at their first appointment – that the breath unconsciously became more shallow and haphazard at times of stress – but that was the first time Casey had ever noticed it in herself.

She took a deep breath, concentrating on it solely. As she did, she suddenly saw that she was repressing a need to cry. She blinked, partly in surprise at the clarity with which she saw this and partly in distress: She didn't want to cry.

She didn't want to hurt. She didn't want to feel that vulnerability right now, and she certainly didn't want to show it to Jessie.

A vague and painful frustration flared through her at this recognition. "Hey Jess, I need to run for a little bit. I'll call you back after while. I just need to – think about this."

"I understand." Jessie's voice was quiet and calm, and Casey had the somewhat uncomfortable feeling she *did* understand. She hung up the phone and leaned against the counter, tears spilling forth like water from a pitcher. It felt that natural, and that irrepressible – like a movement of gravity.

When the crying subsided, she went to the living room and sat on the couch. She tried to pray for Jason or send him healing energy or whatever it was she could do to help him. Instead she found herself restless and unsure how to do any of those things. Choking on a new sob, she fell back against the cushions.

Focusing in earnest, she tried again. She conjured an image of Jason and tried to relax and breathe. With a start, she found herself thinking about the last time he had taken her on the couch on which she sat. She jumped up, feeling horror at the irresistible arousal enveloping her when she had been trying to pray. Biting her lip, she paced around the room, tears again filling her eyes. Suddenly she missed her husband so much she couldn't stand. Wilting to a heap on the floor, she wailed until her body didn't have the energy to cry anymore.

When she next opened her eyes, Casey felt a warmth that seemed to break her heart open. It spread throughout her body, mingling with her pain in a way that felt quite unfamiliar and that she didn't know how to categorize. Suddenly Laurie's question came back to her. *What moves you?*

And then there was an answer. Unbidden and unexpected, it startled her, but she breathed slowly and deeply and stayed with it for a moment.

Sex. Sex was what moved her. Not just the act, but the pure, profound, inherent power of sexuality, that force which encompassed the deepest realms of humanity, spanned the spectrum of life and held within it every possibility of human existence. Sex was life force embodied; it was strength, it was beauty, it was joy, it was –

Healing. Sex was healing. Casey stopped, realizing all she had forgotten. She had forgotten that visceral understanding of sexuality she had had for so long. So divergent from social, cultural, religious messages about sex that at times she had wondered whether it was just utterly skewed, she had eventually allowed that understanding to be subverted, pounded down to the recesses of her subconscious by the relentless permeation of mainstream attitudes about sex.

Now she remembered.

She sat up, recalling how moments before she had felt instantly guilty about thinking of her husband sexually when she was trying to pray for him. Now she slowly let that orientation come back, her breath catching as she remembered the hard, wanting look in his eyes as he grabbed her and pushed her against him, as if he were trying to physically meld them together, and her feeling of their absolute mutual willingness to do that if they could.

Love, she said silently, concentrating on the word – or rather, what the word meant to her. She focused all her energy on love, on summoning it, embodying it, projecting it, and then she pictured Jason. Eyes closed, Casey breathed in love, pulling the energy of it into her being and sending it back out with her exhalation, so that love was what she was moving through the universe, love was why she was breathing at that moment.

Then she moved her hand between her legs.

Holding this concentration, she moved her fingers in circles around her clit, her breathing increasing as she held love in her consciousness and visualized her husband. She came surprisingly fast, gasping as she felt as though love itself was exploding from inside of her as orgasmic energy rushed through her in physical form. She lay in surprise both at how quickly the orgasm had come and also at its power – it wasn't necessarily *more* powerful than her usual orgasms. But it was a *different* power.

She didn't move as she caught her breath, eyes resting on the chandelier on the ceiling above her. There was an exhilaration in her beyond the sexual satisfaction she usually experienced when she made herself come. She had the inarticulable feeling that she had truly just actively manifested love in the universe.

Then she realized what it was. It was prayer. That was the moment Casey realized her personal form of prayer through orgasm. In conjunction with her physical body, through the sacred, luminous, incomparable power of orgasm, she was embodying the intention to manifest the energy she aspired to bring to the universe. What else was prayer than that?

Casey guided her focus to healing. Her fingers still resting on her clit, she began the gentle circular motion again, this time holding the intention of healing for Jason. She was generally multi-orgasmic, but once again she was astonished by how quickly she came, crying out as the energy of healing moved through her as if from somewhere else, as though her body was just the conduit, the building of arousal pulling healing energy in and the orgasm sending it slicing out from her body so intensely she almost couldn't see.

She lay panting, her desire for her husband so strong she felt it racing through her body like an electric current. She looked back at the couch and let the memory come this time: the heat of Jason's touch making her catch her breath as he came up behind her, the stubble of his two-day beard grazing her neck as he whispered in her ear how much he wanted to fuck her. She'd turned, and he'd pushed her onto the couch, ripping at her clothes as her breathing grew heavier and her pussy wetter. He had pushed into her with a voracity that made her cry out, an involuntary sound from deep in her core, the same place she felt the connection with him that took her – took them both – to another plane of existence, a place beyond thought, beyond form, beyond any separation between their physical bodies.

Casey shuddered now as she pictured it, bringing herself to climax once more with the simple memory of that connection; an orgasm just for her this time, beautiful and powerful but personal.

After a while she stood to return to the kitchen. A warm, weightless light seemed to fill her, infusing her simplest movements with a feeling of sacred energy. As she refilled her teacup, the phone rang.

She looked at caller ID and felt her heart crack open. Barely able to speak, she took a deep breath and answered it.

"Hi," her husband said, and the hesitation, fear, and desperation Casey heard in that one syllable overwhelmed her. She dropped against the counter, silent sobs pulsing through her body, and begged the universe with all the might she had for her husband. For his healing, his happiness, and if it were possible amidst those two things, for their reconciliation.

"I was just thinking about you, and – I wanted to see you," Jason's voice cracked in a way Casey remembered hearing perhaps twice in the 10 years she had known him. "There's so much–" his voice halted, and Casey's hand went to her breastbone as she felt the pain in him shoot through her own heart. "There's so much I want to tell you," he finished, his voice unable to hide the tears in it by the time the sentence was out.

Casey breathed. Slowly and consciously. She hadn't seen her husband for three months. At their separation, believing it to be best, she had instigated a "no physical contact" rule that neither of them had yet initiated breaking.

"Can I see you?" Jason whispered.

Casey felt the depth of connection beyond even her capacity to think about it, as simply something known, understood, emanating from her core.

Moving her.

The word slid out as part of her breath, an unbreakable whisper from an abiding stillness: "Yes."

... Then

"Would you grab the gift on the table, please?" I called to Chris as I shrugged into a light jacket and waited for him by the door.

Chris appeared in the foyer a few seconds later, studying the package in his hand. The sparkling wrapping paper was almost blinding as it reflected the setting sun streaming through the window. "It's very... bright," he said, grabbing his own jacket.

"Sarah loves bright things," I reminded him, taking the box from him. I tucked the envelope I was holding under the royal blue ribbon and smiled at the glittering package. "Ready?"

Though the party had only started a half hour before, there were a couple dozen people already filling Sarah and Shawn's house when Chris and I squeezed through the door fifteen minutes later. I set Sarah's present on a table beside the basket filled with various colored envelopes.

"Valerie!" Sarah called my name as she appeared in the crowd and wove through it to greet us.

"Happy birthday," I said as I enveloped her in a warm hug. "Sorry we're a little late." I stepped back and turned to Shawn, who had come up beside her. As he hugged me delicately, careful not to spill the glass of wine in his hand, I caught sight of a tall figure with his back to me standing near the kitchen. As I watched, the figure turned, and the suspicion fueling the low heat forming inside me was confirmed.

It was Hayden.

For a moment my stomach disappeared as the same jolt of arousal sizzled through me that had every time I'd laid eyes on Hayden. I hadn't seen him for a few months – not since Sarah and Shawn's wedding. Looking at him now, I remembered back to that uncomfortable feeling of instability upon first meeting Hayden at their engagement party, the guilt of knowing I was intensely attracted to him juxtaposed with the understanding that I had no desire to leave my relationship with Chris.

I caught my breath as Hayden spotted me. Though much had transpired since that time, my physical attraction to him seemed not to have abated at all. I smiled as he approached, stepping forward to embrace him as we exchanged greetings. Though our hug was casual, the shiver from the pit of my stomach to my pussy as he touched me was both familiar and intense as ever.

I placed my hand on Chris's arm as I backed up. I had introduced the two of them at the wedding, and while I had felt slightly awkward at the time, the brief interaction had seemed cordial. I cleared my throat and re-introduced them, my cheeks – and my pussy – flaming.

Hayden smiled and Chris nodded as the two of them shook hands.

Shawn called Hayden away then. I did my best to catch my breath as I avoided speaking by heading to the food table. I noticed the arousal roiling in the pit of my stomach wasn't so tied up this time with the feelings of guilt and confusion I had experienced when I'd first met Hayden. It was now simply there, a base attraction I felt some degree of relief knowing Chris was aware of.

Of course, he may not have been aware right then that my panties had grown wet when Hayden had touched me. I almost jumped when Chris said, "You look a little flushed."

I looked up to find him studying me closely. I couldn't tell if his tone held a note of awareness or not. His face was impassive as he continued, "Would you like me to get you a drink?"

I nodded and thanked him as I turned and grabbed an hors d'oeuvre. Before he could return, Sarah enlisted my help in the kitchen, and I followed her dutifully, taking a deep breath as I tried to relax.

I refilled a tray of dark chocolate bonbons, only subconsciously scanning the kitchen for a glimpse of Hayden. Placing a mint leaf in the center of the tray, I carried it out to the living room and repositioned it on the food table, then looked around the room for Chris.

I caught sight of him near the patio and made a move to join him before I stopped short. My stomach jumped.

He was talking to Hayden.

Nervousness pressed in around me. There wouldn't be a scene, would there?

It only took a few seconds of observation to see that there was no animosity in the interaction. On the contrary, it seemed as I continued to observe them. The interaction didn't appear exactly casual, but there was no sign of heatedness either. Even from across the room, I could see that neither man's body language displayed indications of hostility or feeling threatened. Hayden's gray eyes were serious, and he nodded a couple times as I watched. Chris clasped Hayden's shoulder as he turned away in a way that looked more meaningful to me than a friendly "Hey, how you doing" kind of gesture.

I had no idea what they had said to each other, but there was something in the interaction I couldn't place, something that seemed unexpected somehow. I turned and headed back to the kitchen, unable to explain the stab of poignancy that slid through me.

Half an hour later I stood with Shawn outside on the patio.

"You may not know this, but Hayden was cheated on once," he said in a low voice, glancing over my shoulder before he continued. "It hurt him a lot. Obviously that didn't happen with you two, but he told me once that when it occurred to him how close he'd come to being on the other side of that scenario, he'd always wanted to apologize to Chris."

I hadn't known. Shawn added, "He knows Chris already knew about the situation, of course. He wouldn't have said anything if he didn't know you two had already talked about it."

It occurred to me then what I had seen in their conversation that I hadn't placed: vulnerability. It wasn't obvious or prominent, but it had been there. The poignancy I'd felt when I'd witnessed their exchange returned more strongly, and my eyes dropped as I imagined what it had taken for Hayden to approach Chris and the graciousness Chris had appeared to exhibit in accepting it.

Chris didn't mention the conversation with Hayden during the rest of the party or on the way home. I wondered if he knew I was aware of it.

When we got inside, he said as he shrugged out of his jacket, "Shawn told me you noticed Hayden and me talking tonight."

I turned to him. "I did, yes."

Chris smiled. "He said he'd mentioned to you what it might have been about. He was right. Hayden was very polite. It seemed pretty cool of him to seek me out like that."

"I'm glad you found it so," I said, sincerely.

The topic dropped. I felt a combination of gratitude and wistfulness wash over me as we headed up the stairs. Though my attraction to Hayden was still strong, the relief I felt at its being out in the open was immense, and the appreciation I felt toward Chris for not finding it threatening was almost fierce.

I reached for him as we entered the bedroom and wrapped my arms around his waist from behind, squeezing as I pressed my cheek against the smooth fabric of his shirt. He chuckled and lifted my hand to kiss it.

"I love you," I said, my voice muffled against his back.

"I love you too," he said, unwinding himself and turning around so he could kiss me on the mouth.

After a few minutes I broke away with a smile and headed for the closet, unzipping my dress as I walked. I opened the closet door and almost dropped my dress when Chris said, "So you're interested in Hayden sexually?"

I froze. That was a trick question if there ever was one. Especially since Chris already knew the answer.

"I – well, yes," I answered finally. "I think you were aware of that."

Chris nodded. "I was just seeing if it was still the case."

I stared at him. His tone was neutral, and I had no idea what his motivation would be for pursuing such a discovery.

"Might I ask why?"

Chris turned to me. His blue gaze was still unreadable, but I felt the undercurrent of lust in it that instantly ignited my own. He didn't say anything for a moment, just stared at me like that, almost as though he were wrestling with something inside himself.

"Maybe it's something I might like to watch."

My jaw dropped. It was a suggestion I would never have expected Chris to make. Granted, one of the things I had found so frustrating around my infatuation with Hayden was that to me, it had never felt like it and my relationship with Chris were even connected – I didn't actually feel a threat to how I felt about Chris in how I felt about and what I wanted to do with Hayden. But convention – and, nonetheless, agreement with Chris – said otherwise, and one of the displeasures of the situation had been the feeling of wrestling with an attraction to Hayden that seemed so strong it felt like it would take me over, thus realistically threatening a relationship with a man I loved despite how arbitrary and unfair that threat seemed to me.

Still, I had never seen any indication from Chris that he had felt anything similar.

"Watch?" I scarcely dared to breathe as I sought confirmation of what he was saying.

"Watch you fuck him. Would you like that?" Chris crossed the room in three full strides, stopping inches from my body as his eyes, ferocious in their lust-filled state, bore into mine.

I looked at him dizzily, almost faint from both the shock and the arousal the suggestion had evoked.

Chris moved a tiny bit closer until he was almost touching me, until I could feel the heat from his body against my vulnerable, naked skin. "Would you?" The demand was calm, a solid, even cover above the simmering desire I sensed beneath it. My fingers reached out and brushed Chris's cock, fully hard now beneath his trousers as he held my gaze. I felt my heart pounding, my breath coming in hot, ragged gasps as I looked up at him.

"Yes."

I expected to feel nervous, anticipated the adrenaline as I stood in Hayden's bedroom. But as my eyes locked with his as he stood near the foot of his bed, all I felt coursing through me was the unadulterated desire I had felt every time I'd looked at Hayden. My body shuddered as I took a deep breath.

I'd asked Chris the night before what he wanted from this. He'd looked thoughtful. "I want to watch you get what *you* want," he'd finally answered. "That's what I want."

Chris sat now in the chair to my left, facing the king-sized bed. I looked over at him. His expectant gaze was dark with lust, accentuating my own as I turned back to Hayden. Suddenly I felt shy, like the star of the show, the sole one the audience (in this case, the audience of two) was here to see.

Then Hayden stepped forward, and the spell in me broke. I met him without pause, closing the distance between us the way I'd wanted to since I'd first laid eyes on him. The air in the room went from anticipatory holding pattern to oxygen in the fire the moment we touched each other, the scene shifting from placid to burning as Hayden's hands found my shoulders, my hair, my neck, my breasts as he kissed me. I forgot everything but the touch I had fantasized about so many times as it trailed sparks now over my physical body. My clothes dropped away as I closed my eyes, feeling my body shake as Hayden's lips pressed fervently along my neck.

I backed up and fell, naked, onto the bed. Still standing, Hayden watched me as he ripped open a condom. I recognized the hunger in his eyes, a reflection of my own that I'd felt so many times upon meeting that silver gaze. I remembered then the night we'd met, how I had later made myself come over and over again imagining that very look in his eyes and how much I wanted him to run it over my naked body.

The recollection took my breath away anew. Impulsively, I turned over as Hayden made a move toward the bed. I heard the duplicate intakes of breath as the inner exhibitionist in me seemed to break free, making me rise to my knees and drop my cheek against the mattress. I arched my back, wanting not only for them to get an unobstructed view of my naked pussy but also for Hayden to enter me that way, the way I'd imagined him doing so many times.

I felt him on the bed behind me. With a primal grunt, Hayden grabbed my hips and pushed into me as I gasped, spreading my knees wider as I felt my own wetness drip down my thighs.

I turned my face to Chris. His straining erection poked out of his open jeans, his eyes fastened to where Hayden's and my bodies connected. The hand resting on his cock held the slightest tension only I would recognize. He was holding back.

His gaze slid to mine, and my pussy jumped at the carnal desire I saw there.

"Spank her," he said suddenly, his voice hoarse. "She loves that."

And that's when I heard it. I knew that pitch, that particular way Chris sounded when he was so turned on he was having trouble keeping his composure. I'd heard it many times, in public, in private, at expected times and unexpected times. But I always knew what it meant.

Any trace of a question I had felt about Chris's comfort or security or desire dissolved when I heard that tone. I let out a shriek as Hayden complied, his hand connecting with my ass as I buried my face in the pillow in front of me, nearly dizzy with lust and desire and ecstasy. Hayden spanked me again, and again, and again, until I was so frenzied I hardly knew what was going on. Then he reached beneath me and brushed my clit, and I gyrated against his fingers frantically as I came, gripping the pillow that muffled my scream.

My body went limp as I finished. Hayden turned me over and knelt between my legs, and I looked up at him, breathing heavily. His gray eyes looked into mine, the heated yearning I had seen in them so many times merging with a carnal satisfaction as he slipped back inside me. I sighed and closed my eyes.

Hayden fucked me slowly as I ran my hands over my breasts. I moved them languidly, feeling my skin in a way more intimate than I ever remembered, connecting with my own body as much as with the other two in the room with me. Suddenly I felt fragile, but not in a physical sense. Lying there naked with Hayden above me, Chris to my left, the caring and respect and openness I knew was in the room, my breath stopped in my throat. I felt tears come forth and didn't know how to hide them.

I turned my head away, unsure if either of them was looking at me. I didn't want them to think I was upset or that something was wrong, and I felt a vague, inexplicable embarrassment at feeling so strongly a way I didn't even know how to describe.

When the tears evaporated, I looked back at Chris. He smiled at me this time, arousal combined with the tenderness and affection of the whole of the three and a half years we had shared together, telling me how much he loved this and how much he loved me all at once. The embarrassment vanished. I realized part of what I was feeling was gratitude, gratitude and a monumental relief that Chris understood this, that he didn't feel intimidated, that he realized that what was happening was no threat to how I felt about him or my commitment to him or our relationship. That it was enhancing rather than diminishing anything.

I closed my eyes, the warmth rushing through my body making me reach out. Hayden interlaced his fingers with mine, and I opened my eyes. He smiled at me, too, the understanding in his gray eyes reflecting some of the same gratitude I experienced. I arched my back, meeting his slow thrusts, and his breath sharpened. I felt myself close to coming again as he lowered his body onto mine, his lips working their way up my neck to my ear.

Goosebumps sprayed over my body as he whispered into it. "Do you know how fucking long I've wanted this, wanted you?" The words seemed to shoot physically through me, my body responding involuntarily as I pushed against him, taking his thrusts deeper as I remembered all the times I had wanted Hayden inside me exactly as he was now, to be spread open below him inviting him to take me however he wanted to. He kept whispering as I came again, the sound that ripped through my voice coming from my very center as he pressed my hands against the mattress, his fingers squeezing mine until I stilled.

My breath shuddered as the climax subsided. Hayden fucked me harder then, rising back up on his knees and grasping my thighs for traction. Out of the corner of my eye I saw Chris stand and approach me in one fluid motion. I turned my head as he reached me, and his cock and my lips met as in a kiss, his flesh sliding seamlessly into the warm, wet haven of my mouth. I looked up at him adoringly, swirling my tongue around his length as he ran a hand through my hair.

Hayden's breath quickened, and his hands clutched me harder. I spread my legs further for him, moaning against Chris as Hayden pounded into me. Chris started to push his cock in and out of my mouth, kneading one of my breasts as his other hand tightened on my hair. Hayden reached up to grip my waist and gasped as he came, thrusting hard as his fingers dug into my flesh.

I closed my eyes as I felt overcome, centering for a moment to take in everything I was receiving. Hayden exhaled deeply as his body jerked, and I opened my eyes, pulling away from Chris for a moment to meet Hayden's silver gaze as I clenched my pussy around him.

I turned and took Chris's cock back in my mouth, knowing both of them were watching me as I sucked it hungrily. Chris thrust a little harder as his breath quickened, and I felt the first spurt of come on my tongue just as Hayden pulled out of me. Chris groaned as he shot his load in my mouth, and I rested a hand on his thigh, swallowing everything he gave me.

Finally he finished. I let his cock fall from my mouth and gave him the same smile he'd given me moments before from across the room.

Hayden, now dressed, sat on the bed as Chris zipped up his jeans. Only I was still naked, lying still under the gazes of both men as the air in the room calmed down once again. Myriad feelings, both expected and unexpected, moved inside me like a kaleidoscope. I hadn't anticipated feeling as close to Chris as I ever had, experiencing a level of trust that was unique, that had never been there before. And I felt an expansion, a freedom evoked not just by sexual satiation but by surrender, the surrender by all three of us to something unknown, something that could seem threatening but that held the potential for something more, something unseen, something I had just experienced and didn't yet know how to describe.

Perhaps most of all, I felt astonished by the groundedness, openness, and self-possession the willingness to even consider what had just transpired had required from both Hayden and Chris. The poignancy I'd experienced seeing them talking at Sarah's party magnified exponentially, and a lump formed in my throat as I marveled at the extraordinariness they had displayed.

Then I remembered what I knew about each man – in one case quite a bit and in the other a strong impression – and it didn't seem so surprising anymore.